D1860257

Tales From Sabz Baug

Tales From Sabz Baug

Anuradha Kalhan

KALPAZ

©Author
All rights reserved. No part of this work may be reproduced, stored, adapted, or transmitted in any form or by any means, electronic, mechanical, photocopying, micro-filming recording or otherwise, or translated in any language, without the prior written permission of the copyright owner and the publisher. The book is sold subject to the condition that it shall not, by way of trade or otherwise, be lent, resold, hired out, or otherwise circulated without the prior publisher's written consent in any form of binding or cover other than that in which it is published.

The views and opinions expressed in this book are author(s) own and the facts reported by them have been verified to the extent possible, and the publishers are not in any way liable for the same.

ISBN: 978-93-5324-957-1

First Published, 2022

Published by

Kalpaz Publications
C-30, Satyawati Nagar,
Delhi – 110052
Ph.: 011-47034999, 9811692060
www.kalpazpublications.com
E-mail: kalpaz@hotmail.com

Printed at: Gyan Press, Delhi.

For

Aijaz Ahmad
With love

Contents

Anacrusis

When the flurry of life abated, I turned to stories.

As it was lived before the Covid-19 virus grounded life to a halt, existence was marked by need to rush, work, meet friends, travel, seek diversions, entertainment. All of it often bordered on a frenzy it appeared because when it all stopped most people could not deal with the silence.

Till it struck I too busied myself. Oftentimes working with data and facts that concerned public policies. As the years rolled, I looked at data with a creeping loss of confidence in its import. There seemed to have arisen a socio-political ecosystem entirely capable of surviving and reproducing without facts. Now and then I give vent to despair in public demonstrations. The last ones being the anti-CAA protest. As the pandemic reemerged it became dangerous to attend protest congregations, particularly if one shared a house with older people. The loneliness was peculiar.

Travel bans isolated us even further. Separating family, friends across cities and continents. When 'stay where you unless necessary' rules trapped me in a home-grown bubble for months on end midst wave after wave of infections, I turned to reading stories, hundreds of them. I realised that I come from a rich living tradition of storytelling. Mythological fiction was popular fiction even in 2021. We have festivals for every season based on mythology; public holidays are based on stories. Epic heroes, Gods and Goddesses are familiar figures in stone, plaster, plastic, glass and on paper. They are everywhere. The story rules. To this day leaders conflating themselves with such stories, hold crowd in thrall as they mix new stories with old. It is a country where only a few concerned themselves with facts and data, cause, and effect. Most just love a good story.

As the second wave of 2021 spread, dangers of a weak public health system lay completely exposed. I read horrifying facts only to know what was happening out of a necessity to stay tethered. The virus took away hundreds of thousands of lives for lack of hospital beds, oxygen, medication. Already during the first wave hundreds of thousands had lost jobs and livelihoods, upending families who walked back to villages all over the country. Private companies sliced labour mercilessly to maintain bottom lines. Truth became unbearable, frightening, noxious almost. Apprehension intensified when it became apparent that we were snared in a double pincer, a clever, infectious, dangerous virus on the one hand and mythmaking as public policy on the other. The second arm of the pincer, as powerful and virulent as the real virus, had grown entirely out of a well told story repeated over four decades about efficiency and vigour of the private sector. In that story the private sector was the audacious, heroic growth engine that made jobs and wealth. We were told that in health-care systems, in educational organisations as in commodity production private, for-profit enterprises created the best outcomes. Some stories, when repeated often enough do have extraordinary power. They enable masses to escape reality and find another enchantment.

But as I read the masters, sometimes over again, I learned that stories can also be a source of edification. They have the power to hold a mirror to the reader. They could be frames for truth in the present, the past and for the future, reflecting culture, traditions, social anomy, atrophy, and change. They could hold an ocean in a drop.

It seemed the right thing to do in the silence of isolation, to try and discover the power of story.

I dedicate these to Aijaz Ahmad with whom I shared all but one as I spun them out through the years of covid inflicted interruption. He had stopped reading fiction, but he replied to some of the stories. He argued about the craft but did not discourage me and that's a lot coming from someone him.

Anuradha Kalhan

1

I am That

Oftentimes, a curious passerby wonders how the name Ruidas came to mark the gate of a large, old stone mansion in Kasba Peth. The neighbourhood does not know either. There is no one who knows the story of Siddharama Ruidas and how he arrived in Kasba. Except perhaps, Kadambari who lives behind the thick stone walls with her two sons and Sangeeta. And even she does not know the entire story.

Long, long ago or at least it seems to be a long time ago because so much has changed so fast since, Siddharama Ruidas stepped out of the river and stood on the banks of Chandrabhaga (as the river Bhima is called in Pandharpur) and looked at the reflection of the full moon on the river. A silver ladder ran up to the moon. He looked at the sky. The night wrapped in velvet was decked in brilliant stars like a seductress. Siddha shivered. A gentle breeze rustled through the sugarcane grass and ruffled the jowar crop. He was fifteen years old today, Ai and Baba had solemnly told him so. They had never marked his date of birth before. He reflected on this moment in his life. All that had passed and all that may follow. Then the spellbinding beauty and serenity of the vision before him filled him with a quietude that was to last a lifetime. He was to recall this moment many decades later when he returned to bury his father and stood at the very same spot in tears. He was to remember it again in Pune on the banks of the river Mutha on a night such as this one. It was the night he died, some say of exhaustion, far away from his village, on his fifty-fifth birthday.

That moment by the river, under the moon, when he turned fifteen, was also a moment that filled him with resolve. Soon the sugarcane crop would be harvested, he thought, and he would be busy all day. He got into a fresh, new set of loose white pajamas, a white shirt, and a Gandhi topi. His father had bought them for him from Solapur town last week for his fifteenth birthday. This Mahashivratri he would fast and meditate alone, all day in front of the small Shiva shrine in his village. He had chosen this way of marking the day when Pashupati Nath united with Parvati. This solemn decision he took on his fifteenth birthday. Next year his father was sending him to the big city of Pune to attend a high school so that he could pass his matriculation exam. Siddha would not only be the first boy in his family, but he would also be the first Shudra boy from his village to do so. His parents had worked hard on their land and laboured on larger landholdings of the upper castes in the village to make it possible.

Many years ago, Baba, as he called his father, had heard a voice at the shrine of Sant Dnyaneshwar Mauli in Alandi that had possessed him. Baba was fond of telling and retelling the story to Siddha, who took so many years coming that Baba was already graying. The story went like this, 'Baba's kinsman Suraj Dada, a boatman, had taken him along the river Indrayani once. Siddha was yet to be born; Ai (Siddha's mother) was still in her mother's home. Baba and Suraj Dada dismounted at the ghat near the shrine and walked up to the splendid samadhi. Baba had heard about the shrine of Dnyaneshwar Mauli who a saint of toilers like them but when he saw the shrine, he expressed much surprise over its grandeur. Suraj Dada informed him that from time-to-time Maratha nobles and Peshwas in Pune had developed the shrine. The royal family of Shinde was maintaining it for a long time and their courtiers had started the custom of carrying Dnyaneshwar Mauli's sandals in a palki from Alandi in the annual 'wari' (gathering) to Pandharpur. Such gatherings happen four times a year but the one on Ashadi Ekadashi (usually June -July) was the biggest. On such occasions hundreds of thousands of peasants and artisans like them used to walk (barefoot sometimes) many miles to the Vitthal temple in Pandharpur. They walked together singing songs in praise of Mauli. The courtiers of the Maratha rulers had joined these processions. Similar processions came with Sant Tukaram's sandals from Dehu near Pune to Pandharpur. Of course,

Baba like everyone else from Pandharpur knew all about these waris. Their family too would gather on such occasions around the Vitthal temple. But he had never seen the shrine in Alandi till Suraj Dada took him there.

On that day many years ago in Alandi, as they walked up the ghats they had met three small boys playing the 'dhol' and singing 'abhangas' in praise of the saint. Older men were coaching them. They were kinsmen, they greeted Suraj warmly and talked for a long time, telling the little boys to stop practicing and wait.

Later Suraj told Baba that these boys would soon be earning alms when the pilgrims arrived. Pilgrims arrived in the tens of thousands. Suraj seemed annoyed by the sight of those little boys. He was silent for a long time and refused to go into the shrine telling Baba to go ahead and look around. Suraj Dada waited near the tall pillar with a two tongued saffron flag fluttering on top.

On the way back Baba too stood near the towering pillar on which the saffron flag fluttered as a beacon to the pilgrims. Suraj was, however, lost in thoughts which seemed to put him in a dark mood. Baba looked up at the pillar, the pillar seemed to reach into the sky and the flag touched the sky or so Baba thought as a 'young boy.' At this point in the narration Siddha used to think that perhaps Baba imagined it so because he was a short, slim man. By the time Siddha was thirteen he was already a head taller than Baba. Ai used to say that Siddha had taken after his maternal grandfather. Ai used to often tell Siddha that he was tall like her father and resembled him in more ways than one. She told him that her father came from a family whose ancestor had served in the British army that defeated the army of the Peshwas near Koregaon Bhima in 1818. That job had catapulted the fortunes of the family dramatically. Their house in the village was large and they had more land than anyone of their caste. Everyone envied them. Ai told him that now-a-days the wrath of the upper caste was upon them. Her father had converted to another faith in rebellion. It consists of direct Shiva worship, no idols, no temple, no priest, no blind faith, no superstitions. Her father recognised no caste. He wore a little Ishtalingam tied around his arm with a black thread. He believed that it would unite him with Shiva when he died, and he needed no priest to perform his last rites.

Under the pillar that day in Alandi, Baba said he heard a voice that seemed to come from the sky, the voice said So'ham, So'ham.... over and over again! What on earth did it mean? Baba had stood still, transported by the reverberating sound that no one else seemed to hear. At some point Suraj Dada started walking towards the boat. In the boat Suraj Dada's black mood had shifted and he told Baba.

'Many years ago, it was the year 1927, I think because later that same year, after I returned to Pandharpur, my mother died in childbirth, and I was orphaned. I don't know how old I was then, but I was old enough to be working on a boat as an assistant. We went up the Bhima River with some passengers who told me of a large gathering of our kinsmen at Koregaon Bhima. There is, I was told, a great man, some leader of our caste who was going to speak. Since then, every year, I have rowed up with passengers on the 1st day of January. I earn some extra money at such times. They talk to me freely since they are kinfolks. One year I took many women there too, but I did not take money from the women. They were like my own mother and sisters. They all talk about a great man called Baba Bhimrao Ambedkar. They used to say that the great man is telling us all to go to school, to educate ourselves and be united against oppression. This was many decades ago, now this is 1950, I am becoming an old man, and still those little boys of our caste are learning to sing and play drums to collect alms. They should be in school! Our boys should be in school. I don't have a son Bhau, but when you have a son, educate him.'

Baba had thought about what it all meant. Most of all he thought about So'ham! What did it mean! Among the older kinsmen in his village, one knew a Brahmin priest, who in turn knew some Sanskrit. The Brahmin needed large amounts of firewood and told the old man to fetch it for him from the forest beyond the village. The old man owed some money to the priest so he did his bidding even though he could barely carry the load, but he took Baba to the priest and requested him to explain the meaning of the sound he had heard. The priest kept them both at a great distance and spoke contemptuously, "So'ham means 'I am that'. It is Lord Shiva's call. But you must be mistaken. Shiv Maharaj will never call out to the likes of you."

But Baba thought about So'ham for many decades while he waited for a son to be born and eventually became a Lingayat like his father-in-law. Only one girl had been born. Then Siddha was born at midnight after a long and agonizing labour, Ai almost died. There was no hospital or doctor at hand. Only an old lady in the neighbourhood who was usually called upon for births. At this point in the story Baba would stop and wipe a tear. No matter how many times he told the story, he would shed a tear. "Without your Ai, I would be incomplete, she is my *ardhangini*," he used to say. On that night while Baba waited for Seetha to be born, he thought of the Alandi pillar, the flag that touched the sky and So'ham yet again. He prayed to Shiva to save Ai and the baby. The night Siddha was born Baba also started to worry about saving money for his education. That year Siddha's older sister Girija was to be married off; she was eighteen and already considered too old for marriage by his kinsfolk. The expenses of finding a suitable boy meant that Baba had to take a loan from Deshpande the local Brahmin moneylender against the mortgage of his small land holding. Whatever was left after the sugarcane was sold was only enough to buy them some food and necessities for the year. Ai and Baba started to work as farm hands on other, larger farms for wages. Wages were often paid late or at rates lower than promised. Baba would then habitually worry about the interest payments to the moneylender who was also the largest landlord. Soon Ai was working for no wages on the moneylender's land, the moneylender told Baba he was adjusting it against late payment of interest. But the interest payments kept mounting. Besides, both Baba and Ai were illiterate, they could not keep accounts or calculate the interest rate.

At this point in his narration Baba would pause and rub his palm over his balding head in an agitated way, for a long time. As though relieving the anxiety of those years. Then he would resume the story somewhat like this,

"Salvation came to us at last, in 1973. A local district collector, may God bless him, was investigating the cause of rising farmer suicides in their village. I knew that many of my kinsmen were indebted, droughts in the past years had ruined many, then marriages and funerals took whatever was left. The majority had lost land to the moneylender. Many had to leave the village for towns like Sholapur, Pune and Nasik looking for work. Two, three had returned to tell of their misfortunes in those towns. Finally, some officers of the government in Delhi were implementing a new policy to eradicate poverty, or so I was told by my kinsmen. They had tracked down moneylenders in the district and Deshpande's name had come up. When the learned officers scrutinised his account books, they found much amiss. Deshpande had over a hundred bonded workers. Debt bondage and cheating! Charges were framed against him, and he was arrested. Baba got back his land and renewed his efforts to save. Meanwhile Siddha at the age of ten along with seven other shudra children were enrolled at the village school with the help of local sarpanch who wanted to impress the new district collector. Six of them dropped out within two years but Siddha was a hard-working student, he studied through the night with an oil lamp, and he was promoted rapidly, in fact, every six months." At this point Baba's narration would pause.

Siddha was old enough to know and remember the rest. The local upper caste boys were jealous of him. Their parents too kept a jaundiced eye on him. The school had only two teachers who taught everything up to class five, one of them was kindly disposed to him. Then Baba would resume his story, "One day the kindly teacher, may God Bless him, met me in the market and warned me in a soft voice to take you away from the village. Send him to Pune to complete high school, he said. He will be secure in a big city; he will be safe from the taunts and jibes of the upper caste boys. After 1977, violence against lower castes has increased. Specifically, those who had got back their land and had their debts written off earlier. Pune is the city of Jyotirao Govindrao Phule and his fellow thinkers. I know a family by the name of Bavalkars there, they will house and help Siddha. I will give you a letter that Siddha must take for them and I will also write and post one to them myself." 1977 was the year Siddha was sent off to Pune with the letter at the age of sixteen. Baba came to drop him off. They traveled by bus, and it took several hours because the bus broke down mid-way. Siddha remembered the journey vividly. It was the first of many such.

In Pune, Siddha discovered another world. He learned about Gandhiji and Jawaharlal Nehru, about Mahatma and Savitribai Phule, he read Ambedkar, he read all about the Bhakti saints Tukaram and Dnyaneshwar. He read local newspapers and wrote letters home explaining what he was learning. These letters were read to his parents by the local postman and kept safely in a muslin cloth. Like Jude the Obscure Siddha had struggled with Marathi letters and numerals all alone, in an obscure village. But this Jude was somewhat luckier. It took him three years to get to the tenth grade and pass the matriculation exam. He learned some English, Mathematics, Science, History, Geography. He worked as hard as he could, by day and by night. He worked with a resolve.

Siddha stood first in the matriculation examination in the entire Pune district. His photograph standing beside the Bavalkars appeared in all the local Marathi newspapers, most of them were accompanied by a long write up about his caste and humble origins. Many wrote about the Bavalkars and Jyothiba and Savitribai Phule's mission. He was nineteen when he finished school and returned home to a hero's welcome. The extended family came to greet him, their joy was no less than if he had been the first man on moon Seetha thought ruefully. It was 1980.

Baba was old, bent, and completely bald when Seetha returned; Ai was much younger than him, but she was unable to work on the farm because her back hurt too much. Seetha stayed for a month in the village, then one day he asked his brother-in-law to mind the fields, locked the house and took his bewildered parents to Pune. He did not want to be a farmer anymore. He told them that a small farmer's life was too difficult and precarious. Ai and Baba did not argue.

While in school in Pune Siddha had lived with the kindly family of Bavalkars. They had a house not far from Mahatma Phule wada.

The family consisted of an old couple and their middle-aged, unmarried son who was a teacher in the municipal school. Over generations the family had been followers of Phule. They tried to help the cause of education as best as they could. They treated Siddha well. They gave him food, boarding and lodging. In return he watched over a small hardware shop they had in Bhavani Peth and helped with the household chores after school.

Bavalkars had urged Seetha to return to Pune for they had grown rather fond of his quiet, steady, thoughtful ways. They needed him for the shop. They wrote to him urging him to return. Besides, his attachment to Pune was intensified by fair, gray eyed Kadambari. She was his sprightly, energetic classmate and dear friend. They shared books, class notes and took the matriculation exam together. Kadambari was gleaming with pride when she showed him his photograph in the newspaper. She cared little for the first class she had got. She read out the newspaper reports to anyone who cared to listen. In fact, if he went by the looks people gave him it appeared that she had read it to the entire neighbourhood. Each time she read it aloud to someone in front of him Siddha looked at her rather than at his photograph. Her eyes sparkled with joy. He sensed that there was hope for him there, far greater than the five minutes of fame that newspapers had got him.

Kadambari was the daughter of a poor Brahmin widow Jayanti, who sold wada pao, sabudana kichdi, poha and tea near Bavalkar's shop. Handloom workers and other toilers walking to or from work in the early hours of the morning were her main customers. Kadambari managed the kitchen before and after school while her mother handed out the food, kept accounts, refused credit, scolded the drunks, abused the rough elements, dealt with the police and municipal authorities while she stood tall and stern at the counter in her colourful, nine-yard saree tucked between her legs, kumkum, mangal sutra and plastic slippers all in place. Kadambari was not to appear in front of strangers, her mother had warned her against it.

Mother and daughter were entrepreneurs of a rare kind. Businesswomen were not a common sight in those days. They had arrived in Bhavani Peth one morning from Talegaon, ten years before Siddha arrived. As soon as her husband died of an unknown ailment his family began mistreating Jayanti. Their harsh words and cruel ways quickly burned her heart to cinders and Jayanti ran away. After her husband, it had become apparent to his brothers that Jayanti would not just be a dependent but also a claimant to the family home, lands, and wealth. Newspaper reports about laws confirming a wife's rights in the husband's property were a great source of consternation to them, they discussed it in whispers endlessly behind closed doors. One night, she eavesdropped at the door. They were talking about some Hindu Code Bill and women's rights in property, then they began conspiring to send her on a pilgrimage and giving her daughter up for adoption. She thought of returning to her parent's home. But her parents were too old and poor to support her and a child. Jayanti had wept alone in her room. Above and beyond the ignominy of it all was the rage she felt! Her parents had spent a fortune at her wedding. Then one-night, Jayanti, taking courage in her hands, left her husband's home. She took with her own gold jewellery, some fine clothes that her mother had given her and Kadambari, who was barely five years old. For the first time in her life, she faced the world alone.

As she grew up in Bhavani Peth, Kadambari lost all memory of the past, her father, family wealth, caste, and status unlike the mother who would not fail to evoke the past. Kadambari was a child of the urban chawl. She had grown up in the neighbourhood, all her play mates were from the poor working-class vicinity. Only her mothers' insistence had kept her in school. Unlike all her playmates she had stayed in school. Her friends were all either helping their mothers with housework or were married off before they turned sixteen. If their circumstances required it, as they often did, they went to work for wages. But they all dropped out of school, much to Kadambari's disappointment. A good many went to work as domestic workers in Pune. Their lives diverged but the bonds remained. When they found time, which was rare, they met in Kadambari's two room house near the food stall. While Kadambari cooked they chatted and laughed. Eventually, she was the only girl in the chawl to complete high school. She was by no means the sharpest. Kadambari knew that Sangeeta was the brightest of them all.

No girl in the vicinity had passed school let alone with a first class in living memory. Even her mother was barely literate but was so delighted that she bought Kadambari a new saree, gold jewellery, decorated the shop with buntings and flowers and served free food all day. Hard work, prudence and planning had made Jayanthi a fairly prosperous entrepreneur. When she arrived, she had sold some of her gold to rent a stall and a house in Bhavani Peth. In a few years she had moved out of the makeshift food stall to a small shop opposite the Bavalkars shop in Bhavani Peth. Only a year before her matriculation, on Kadambari's insistence, Jayanti had hired a helper in the kitchen to free Kadambari from cooking and cleaning chores. The hired help was Kadambari's friend, Sangeeta whose parents had pulled her out of school in the fifth grade much to Kadambari's anguish. They had wept together about it. Sangeeta had stood first in the fourth grade. But her alcoholic father used to take all the money that her mother made as a domestic worker. Her five younger siblings ran around hungry and unwashed on the street till the mother or Sangeeta returned. One day, using her network, her mother put Sangeeta to domestic work in the most prosperous home in Kasba Peth. Kadambari could still remember the day she had come to school to take Sangeeta away, never to return. Mercifully Sangeeta's alcoholic father died before long, and her mother could breathe more freely.

Thus, in 1979 the trio, Jayanti, Kadambari and Sangeeta stood poised to make a bigger success of the eatery together and they thrived. Jayanthi had agreed to take on Sangeeta on the promise that Kadambari would continue her education and get some training as an accountant. Kadambari worked but went to night college to get a degree. Sangeeta handled the kitchen and Jayanti the counter. Siddha toiled in the shop while he waited patiently for Kadambari.

When Siddha returned to Pune with his parents, he rented a room near the Bavalkars shop and resumed work, this time on wages. After the shop was closed in the evening, he worked night shifts in the handloom factory to save money. At six o'clock every morning Kadambari waited upon him while he ate breakfast at Jayanti's little restaurant. Then he hurried home to sleep till eleven when he opened the hardware shop. But before he left, he would often reach out shyly, hold Kadambari's hand gently and tell her, "I envy you. I cannot afford to go to college, but you go and study for both of us and bring me back books from your library." He would give her a slip of paper with names of authors on them and she would grimace. He found time to read so many dreary books on history and science but so little time for her. She had cut off her waist long hair to shoulder length, but he had not noticed her fashionable hairstyle. He hardly ever noticed the new sarees she wore in a modern way. She had learned to wear them draped around unlike her mother who wore nine yards of it, between her legs and tucked behind. Siddha only noticed her eyes and face. If she was tired or unwell, he would know immediately. He had not even once told her that she was beautiful. Laxman Rao, her college mate, had written a letter to her the other day describing her beautiful long brown hair and gray eyes. He said that they entranced him. She had cut her hair in a strange reaction to that declaration which she now secretly lamented. Perhaps Siddha liked her long hair better. Yet Seetha had not asked her anything about it. Did he even he noticed it? She felt too shy to ask him.

Exasperated, one day she told him that she was envious of the books because he loved them. Siddha flushed with pleasure, laughed, and replied, "I will read these books once, maybe twice if they are good, but I will hold your hand till I die." That day Kadambari told her mother that she would marry Siddha and no one else. Jayanti was undecided. She kept silent on the issue for days. Till Kadambari could bear it no more.

"Ai, why are you so silent about Siddha? You used to like him and praise his dedication. He made the entire district proud and at that time you were beaming with joy. All the newspaper journalists who came to Bhavani Peth to interview him, did so in your restaurant. Your restaurant was in so many pictures as the place that nourished Siddha. Is it because he is poor or poorer than us now?" Jayanthi had just bought a new house with three rooms near the Vithoba temple, in Bhavani Peth. She bought it in her own name, signing as Smt. Jayanti Mohan Kulkarni. So far, through all her days of lonely struggle she had no use for her surname. Quickly the upper caste people of the area started calling on her and visiting her restaurant. The old temple priest came to perform a pooja in the new house on her invitation. On that occasion the old friends from the chawl were invited but Kadambari noticed many things, the awkward silence between the new and old neighbours, the leering look of the priest as he gaped at her young friends in their best finery, the silent separation in which Seetha sat with his parents. In the months that followed there was a parting of ways between the old friends and the new. Their restaurant received large orders from rich customers. They hired more girls as workers. Sangeetha struggled to manage the small kitchen floor space as the seniormost worker. The entire development made Jayanthi richer but Kadambari and Sangeeta quite miserable.

Jayanti did not talk about Siddha and Kadambari respected her too much to question her further. She continued meeting Siddha in the restaurant and outside, visited his parents frequently, helping them with household and marketing chores. She resolved to marry him after finishing college and when she got a job. At that point in the future, she felt she would be able to confront her mother again.

A few years passed in this manner and yet Jayanti had not spoken a word about Siddha. In these years her grandparents from both sides had discovered them, so had sundry relatives who passed through Pune. Jayanti's success caused much long-lost affection to reappear in their manner even as they speculated outrageously about how a single mother could do so well. They gossiped among themselves, yet they brought many proposals of marriage for the fair and now, well to do, Kadambari. Jayanti was not a gullible innocent anymore, so she treated them all courteously but with a certain cynicism. Kadambari noticed that with some relief. One day an offer of marriage came from an enormously wealthy real estate business family in Pune. Their son

Laxman Rao was smitten with Kadambari. Jayanti was beside herself in shock which soon turned to excitement and temptation. She took Kadambari in her arms and said breathlessly, “This is an opportunity of unimaginable advantage, it is an opportunity to transform your destiny, your world, the future of your children. I have no interest other than yours at heart when I say this. I have struggled all my life to live with some dignity and will continue to do so but you can become a queen!”

That night Kadambari told her mother that she would run away if she was forced to marry anyone but Siddha. And so, matters stood still for a few months till a dumbfounded Jayanti recovered her composure. She was disappointed about Kadambari marrying a poor, low caste boy but eventually she capitulated. She was a practical creature. She had lost her caste and status once in her life and would rather lose it all again than lose her only child. Besides without Kadambari’s accounting and Sangeeta’s management Jayanthi would not survive, she was now too old to manage the enterprise alone. Sangeeta would leave if Kadambari was forced to leave. Seetha and Kadambari were married in court, very simply, with the family and Sangeeta as witness. Kadambari wore a cotton saree, flowers in her hair, she wore no jewellery, no make-up. She thought Siddha would like that. Siddha was delighted with her decision. No religious ceremonies were allowed by the couple.

Eventually, Seetha bought the hardware shop from Bavalkars on easy installments, they had no one to manage it. He worked day and night to pay them off and make a success of the enterprise. He hardly slept, took no care of his own wellbeing, and toiled away as he was accustomed to. The struggle was staggering but he had resolved never to be precarious like his parents and he persevered. Kadambari with Jayanthi and Sangeeta’s help managed to expand the eatery in Bhavani Peth. It became a popular restaurant in Pune. That is how the Ruidas family came to accumulate enough wealth to buy a house and live in Kasba Peth, where thus far, only Brahmins could live.

They lived there for many years with their two sons, donated half their profits to a school in Pune and built a hostel specially for rural children. By night Siddha tutored the rural children, gave them books to read, lectured them every Sunday against superstition, on the necessity of rational thought and empathy. He used stories to make an impact. He involved his sons in the upkeep of the hostel. When Kadambari pleaded with him to rest he would hold her hand and laugh,

> "You, Baba and Ai have given me so much love that I will burst if I do not share it." Kadambari had no argument against Siddha's web of words, she had never been good with words. She would walk away with a heavy sigh, full of longing for his attention. About his love for her she had no doubt all her life. Many years passed thus in tacit commitment.

They had all become defiant Lingayats like Baba. Before he died, he told Siddha, "I now know that Lord Shiva had called out to me in Alandi." Baba wanted to be buried in a seated posture, lingam in palm, on his own land in Pandharpur. A trishul marks the site to this day. Ai is buried beside Baba and Siddha is buried between them. Girija waters the tamarind tree near the graves and everyone who passes by knows the story of Siddha.

2

Catalexis

Six rivers flow through Ahmednagar District yet it is often on the verge of drought.

We live in Jeur, where river Sina begins. Jeur is in tehsil Nagar, district Ahmednagar. The town of Ahmednagar is about sixteen kilometers away. Our village is surrounded by fields of blackish grey soil and dotted with wells. Tall sugarcane, wheat, soyabean and onions crop grow in the winter. The sun shines bright on the crop rippling in gentle breeze as we cycle to school and back. Different kinds of smoke rise from the chimneys in the village, from homes and thick dark fumes from the brick kilns further away. Men and women go about their work all day in the fields. Women return to work at home. The unending churning of mills sometimes grinding wheat and sometimes sugarcane, bellowing of cattle, buzzing of bees and chirping of birds, these sounds give rhythm to our quiet lives. The sharp honking of a passing truck on the highway far away can startle a cow from her reverie. A gentle breeze carries the smell of ripening crops. White fleecy clouds drift across the sky till monsoon arrives and they return as dark laden masses. The seasons changes and so do the crops but the sun always shines long and bright. All through the year it shines, except in the monsoon when thick clouds bring rain and hide it for a few months. Everyone, not just the farmers, wait for rain with increasing eagerness through the hot dry season. The river is not far away but as the dry season progresses it dries up, ponds and wells dry up, the fields look bare, vegetables became scarce, and it seems that the monsoon is the only topic that grown-ups talk about. Life and all activity slow down and then get suspended till it arrives.

We sit, all three of us sisters with Bilkis Phuppo in the inner courtyard of our home. Monsoon clouds hovered above; a gentle, moist breeze stirred not just the mango trees around the house but our hearts with some strange, looming, excitement. We have one sturdy swing hanging off a Peepal tree among the five of us, but yesterday I had taken Hamid chacha's help to tie an old tire I found on the pucca road nearby with a strong rope from the branch of the neem tree. I would not need to wait for the swing to be free of the boys now. My eyes drifted over the mango trees. Alas! They were naked of fruit that we along with our army of cousins had plucked raw off the lower branches and later ripe from the branches higher up. We usually ate them before getting down from the tree to avoid competition. I stood up to see if the swing on neem tree was visible from the inner courtyard.

Bilkis Phuppo raised her eyebrows and voice. "Where is your mind wandering again, Musarrat?" she asks. I sit down hurriedly and try to divert her annoyance with a question that has just occurred to me. I called her Bua like my friends called their aunts.

"Why did Abba name me Musarrat, Bua? What does it mean?"

"It means pleasure," Bua answered slowly with a frown.

Bilkis Phu was a tall, sizeable, serious-minded woman. She wore round glasses on a round, brown face. She wore her saree clumsily, it reached only her claves but always covered her head. She was making us girls learn by rote, we were learning the names and deeds of our male ancestors. Fourteen generations of them. This gathering with Bua usually followed the Quaran lessons that Maulvi sahib gave us once every week on Friday afternoon. But Friday was the one evening we had time to spare. Our days were crammed with school, prayers, mathematics, and Urdu tuitions. My youngest sister Sidra was leaping ahead of us all in memorizing the Arabic text in the holy book. She did not know what it meant yet, but she could recite it. She was praised in family gatherings. I was the slowest of three sisters. Bua did not take long to tell the company. My older brother Haider was considered the star pupil in all respects, he was admired in the family of uncles, aunts, and cousins in the neighbourhood so numerous that I could not total on my fingers. The girls were mostly admired for their mastery of the holy book and obedience. In the last science exam, I had scored the highest in my class and nobody mentioned it. Only father patted me on the head and told mother. Bilkis Bua overheard and frowned.

Last Friday, Bua was telling us that our great grandfather was the tehsildar of Shridi in the days that Sai Baba a holy man, roamed the streets for alms. She mentioned fleetingly that grandmother would cook separately for him, vegetables, and daal. She made sure that no meat touched the grain. She knew which days of the week he came to their village, and waited anxiously to see him with her children, she would give him food and would ask him to bless her children. It was in no small measure that Sai Baba's blessings have helped the family through good times and bad times said Bua. The girls were all looking up with great interest but this part of the story she rushed through, and Bua went back to the men and their deeds. The men seemed ordinary enough to me. Farmers and wholesale dealers in grains and edible oils. Hard working and frugal. Most had made money, bought land, shops, and had generally prospered. Bua knew the size of land and number of shops they bought. My father was the first to go to law college and become an advocate. All the kasbah came to him for advice and guidance. As population, land and business disputes mounted, he was the busiest man in our world with an office in the town nearby. He was hardly ever at home. Bua remarked on his education and business with uncertain wonder.

"Why do we have to learn their names, none of my school friends have to waste their Friday afternoons like this, they can play in the fields." I had wondered aloud one Friday with unconcealed irritation. Bua was exasperated, she frowned at me as she often did and said rather loudly "You are getting ruined in that wretched school. Don't they teach you that no generation can prosper without the blessings of the previous generations." I was never at loss for words and always a little fearful that I would be taken out from school at Bua's advice. I lied promptly, "Of course they do but only in secondary school, they let the small children like us play."

Then she told us that our forefathers had come to this district of Ahmednagar in Maharashtra with the Mughal army. Our early ancestors were Pathans of Pashtun ethnic ancestry from the Northwest of the subcontinent. They came as commanders and soldiers in the army of the emperors who wanted to conquer and retain the Deccan. They spoke a different language then called Pashto. Their armies were stationed here for so many decades that the soldiers married locals and remained. That part of history was lost, we did not know their names or their deeds of valour because the habit of memorizing was not formed nor were the graves marked. "That is why we are different from others around us, there are Pathans like us scattered all over the district" she said pensively. We did not understand what she meant. We only saw the 'others' in school actually. We were not very different at all. I thought we looked same as them. We spoke the same Marathi language in school and home, but we learned Urdu at home, they did not. We ate meat but so did everyone else except the Brahmin children. They ate it, nonetheless, said they did not eat it. I know that because they shared our food with enjoyment. Bilkis Bua's mutton korma was a special hit. She had started adding coconut to it and everyone in school liked it. I hardly got to eat any if I took it to school. One day I took kebabs to school and my friend a Brahmin girl called Meena asked me what kind of meat it was. I said it could be anything cow, goat, deer, rabbit I didn't know. She ate it nevertheless and asked for more. I realised then that I had to tell Bua to put extra food in my lunch box.

So, it was that I could never tell the difference between others and us.

The girls in our family were often dusky and the boys light skinned but there were plenty of exceptions. The boys of our family were very tall and muscular, a foot above the others. But I noticed that fact only when were ready to leave school and move to college. And in college, in Pune, I was told categorically by new friends that Brahims do not touch meat and they venerate the cow. I was filled with guilt for my folly of feeding my childhood friends so much beef.

Of the girls, I was the oldest and Sidra was five years younger, Siama was 4 years younger than me. We were dispatched to school one by one by my father. It was a coeducation school which was considered better than the other schools close by. He taught us to ride bicycles. He did all this against the advice of Bilkis Bua. Father told Bua that in 1970 AD to think like 1870 AD was not tolerable in any sensible religion or culture. None of us knew what he meant but his word was law, and we were glad for it. Bua kept quiet on the issue but kept an eagle eye on our activities, dupatta, and complexion. If we had spent too much time in the sun or our legs ached, she would know and she would frown.

Bua was actually father's Bua and so my grand Bua, she was widowed early in life. Her sister, Choti Bua Amira, was also a widow. The two lived with us. Amira was fifteen years younger than Bilkis Bua, she was the extraordinary beauty of our family but sadly widowed a day after she got married. She was childless but refused to remarry despite many offers Bilkis Bua told us. Amira Bua was habitually quiet and caring of everyone's needs. I do not remember a time when the two were not in the house with us. Father would treat them with much affection and respect, and he never let them return to their married home in the villages nearby. In return both the Bua's would indulge his sons and keep an eye on us. Bilkis Bua would scold us girls and advice mother on various matters pertaining to tradition and religion with respect to girls. All the advice was merely to improve us she reminded us, every day. We took her frowns well enough because she was a marvelous cook and made many treats for us and our friends. Bilkis Bua knew which dish each one of us liked and disliked. Both the Buas would eat their meals with us after we came back from school. Both stitched our clothes from a big spool of cloth, they did so twice a year before Eid, the same fabric for boys and girls. Everyone got two white salwars and pajamas. The girls got colourful kurtas and dupattas. In addition, they gave us all generous sums of money as Eidi. The same amount to boys and girls. It was the only money we ever got as children which father took from us and put into a post office saving account much to our dismay. They knitted our cardigans, socks, and mufflers every winter for the next winter, casting off and casting on stitches, calling us in to hold the knitting against us for size as they sat in the inner courtyard talking and taking the sun. Even that was done in same-coloured wool. Hamid Chacha went on his old scooter and bought it for them every year from Ahmednagar town. It was only much later when my brothers began to get teased by their school friends for wearing gulabi rang and sabz rang sweaters that this practice stopped. Everyone got to choose the colour. I chose red every year.

Mother was not in charge of the household she was their helper, no more. But all in all, I suspect that it was an amicable, harmonious arrangement for mother was not an energetic woman. Having produced two sons and three daughters she tired easily, fell ill in every season with a different ailment particular to the season, and greatly appreciated the chance to rest frequently in a quiet, darkened room during the day.

When I was about eight years old father bought a handsome black ambassador car. It stood outside our home, at first all the cousins, uncles and aunts came to see it and then the one by one the rest of the village came. It stood stationary for three months, father still walked everywhere or rode a cycle as did the rest of us. Hamid chacha took to washing it every day because sometimes people from the adjoining village also came to congratulate father and Bilkis Bua was fond of showing off to them.

Haider my oldest brother was soon eighteen and he was to leave home to study in a medical college far away. We stood outside, Haider's trunk was packed, and a hold all had his blanket and mattress. Haider was wearing a new pair of trousers and shirt. Father had a whole new set of clothes stitched for him for the first time by a professional tailor in the town. The preparations for his departure went on for a month. Bilkis Bua cried the most, she could not understand why Haider could not become a farmer or trader like his uncles and stay near home. Father tried to tell her that Haider would return after he finished his studies. It was only then that all the women and servants stopped crying, but they began all over as soon as the luggage was loaded in the car.

Father was to drop Haider off at the Ahmednagar railway station with Hamid Chahcha who was to accompany him to

Nagpur as father had an important court matter coming up and could not go to Nagpur.

When father tried to start the car, it would not budge. Much excitement followed; the chorus was there are only two hours for the train to start. Nobody, least of all fathers knew what to do with the car. Hamid chahca opened the bonnet. He muttered something about engine, said something about battery. This went on for half an hour then he jumped on his scooter and went off to get a tonga that could carry the luggage to the nearest bus stop.

Just then an uncle, Nur mamu arrived from Nagar. He had come to see the car. He had heard about it from another cousin. Father greeted him ruefully from a distance and told him that the car was of no use.

"Is it a secondhand car?" asked Nur mama.

"No, its brand new," said father. Nur mamu opened the bonnet poked around, then got behind the wheel and started it. The operation lasted 5 minutes. A shout of relief rented the air. I clapped loudly only, then realised that I had stepped forward and was looking keenly at what he was doing and then I followed him into the car. I looked at Nur mamu with newfound respect. That day Hider, Abba, Nur mamu, Hamid chacha and I went to the railway station in the back car in prodigious style.

Nur mamu became by favourite relative. Few years later I heard that he and his three sons has started a garage to repair automobiles. They had acquired such a reputation that people came from far and wide. When I was in high school, I had to move to another school closer to the city. I once asked Nur mamu if he would take me to the garage. He agreed readily.

That simple request of mine set off a skirmish at home. All the women were aghast. How could a mature girl have such a desire they asked each other. They spoke to me in turn and together. They wanted to know what I wanted to do in a place where only men went. When father returned from the city, they told him what I had said to Nur mamu. Bilkis Bua spoke as though I had murdered someone. Father did not say anything to me, but everyone treated me differently for a few days after that.

I spoke to my new school friends Vaidehi Deshmukh and Sangeeta Kumble about it. They were more than sympathetic. They said they faced endless criticism from the women in their own homes for expressing simple wishes like going to a Fair in the next village or taking a boat ride by themselves. The censure was followed by threats of marriage, and they were barely 15 years old! At least that did not happen to me, I thought. We exchanged notes frequently thereafter. One day, on the eve of our final examination we swore to fight back against oppression of all kinds. We wrote it on a paper, made three copies and signed it. Each of us got a copy to keep. I still have mine in a locket around my neck. The memory of that pledge brings a smile to my face to this day.

As it happened, one day after the final exams father came home early, it was barely afternoon. That had become a rare occurrence after he joined the local unit of the Indian National Congress party. He had told us he could not refuse because none other than the Chief Minister of the state had approached him for his support. They had come to him in 1992 based on his reputation as a lawyer and progressive member of his community. They told him they needed his help in the trying times ahead. I was old enough to have heard about the riots between Hindus and Muslims after a mosque was destroyed somewhere far away. There was tension in Ahmednagar too father had said. Bua had started praying more fervently for his safety. She already prayed for Haider and Shakeel she later added my name and those of my sisters to the list of people for whom prayers would be read. As we left home for college one by one, she became more and more religious.

That day after lunch, father took me to his room and shut the door. He asked me what I wanted to study in college. I had never even thought about the matter. I asked him if Bua would allow me to go since Haider had not returned to the village and Shakeel who was younger to Haider had also gone away to Pune to study law.

I was the eldest girl, and it would set a precedence that could not be repudiated. Father listened to my bitter tone, wiped an angry tear from my cheek, patted my head, and told me to rest assured that I could study whatever I liked.

I spent the summer vacation reading Marathi newspapers and magazine that father brought home. I was often thinking of what I wanted to study when I was helping Bua in the kitchen or with the stitching. I discussed it with Haider and Shakeel who came home for Eid. I had to be clear headed and determined or father would be embarrassed for having always supported me so open-handedly. None of my numerous friends had such a tower of strength in their lives.

After my brothers left home, father sensed that both the Buas and mother were gloomy. Once a fortnight, on a weekend, father took us all in the ambassador car for a drive. A huge picnic basket with roti and kebabs, halwa, fruits and tea were packed. Preparations for the picnic lasted for two days before the appointed day. We were all tall girls now, I sat in front with father, my sisters sat on mother's and Bua's lap bent over to fit in. We went to the city with our heads properly covered. Bua insisted on heads being covered now that we were grown up. I did not like that. I thought that it made us different from other girls of our age in the village. In the city it made us dreadfully conspicuous. Girls were very fashionable in the city, their clothes and their hair made into elaborate braids, with colourful clips and buns or left flying about in the breeze. I had only seen such girls on the TV we had just acquired and that too was switched off as soon as it got interesting. We were never permitted to decorate ourselves for outings! Father took us to the historical monuments in Ahmednagar and told us their legend. It was Chand Bibi dargah and its tale that caught my attention. He took us to the Ahmednagar Fort and mother who was often silent suddenly piped up and said "Pandit Nehru was imprisoned here, and he wrote a famous book." We looked at mother in surprise. How do you know we asked her in one voice?

"My father as a young man used to come here in visiting hours to meet him, he was member of the Congress and a freedom fighter," she said simply. And because we kept looking at her flushed face and shining eyes she added.

"He too was in jail for many years, and I was barely ten years old when he died of some illness. My mother could hardly cope with us children. I was the youngest and only eighteen when a suitable proposal came for me. Amma said this family shares your father's values, you will be happy, but I am sorry I cannot educate you further." Bilkis Bua held my mother's hand and kissed it. We went around mother and hugged her.

I saw the hustle and bustle of the city. It thrilled me. Most of all the buses and automobiles moving about excited me. Mother said the automobiles stink. Bua said they made her deaf. All the women collapsed when they got back home and swore, they would not go again till the next trip was organised and they were given no choice.

One day an ugly incident occurred that left me dumbfounded. Father had taken us to Emperor Aurangzeb's tomb who had died in Ahmednagar district. A simple, two-tier grave had been erected in stone and a small, paved yard stood around it. Father told us about his religious piety and rigidness. He spoke to us at length about his brother Crown Prince Dara Shukoh and the political tussle that brought Aurangzeb to the throne. I knew that father had been reading Dara Shukoh's 'Sakinat ul Auliya' and 'Safinat ul Auliya'. Then he asked me read to from an Urdu Book of Sufi verse. It was a wonderful moment of tranquility. My voice carried far into the open space, a light breeze sprung up and shards of sunlight bounced off the pages of the book in my hand. As I turned the page Bilkis Bua noticed that it was time for the maghrib namaz. Father spread the mat for her and all of us kneeled, for some reason even father who was careless about his prayers. It so happened that we were facing the west and at the same time facing Aurangzeb's tomb. Just then someone hurled a tomato that landed on Haider and yelled "Oye! Babur ki aulad go to Pakistan." Hamid was so deep in prayer that he did not look up. I did and caught sight of three young men with thick bamboo sticks and orange marks on their brows. I stared at them and did not flinch when they jeered, they left. Nobody moved. Later Hamid washed his back of the residue of the tomato. And father said these were ignorant men encouraged by deceitful leaders. Otherwise, no decent human being left to himself behaved like this. Bua asked Allah to forgive them all and show them the right way. And we left in silence.

In those days we visited the district dams, rivers, monuments, and father taught me to drive. He also took me to Nur mamu's garage. My cousin brothers were all at work on the cars, trucks, vans parked all around the garage. Their enterprise had prospered. A new car called Maruti had come to the city in large numbers and my cousins were eagerly discussing its design and components. I was fascinated. I could drive now but not without father for I did not have licence and we never told Bua.

When summer vacations ended, I told father that it would give me great pleasure to study automobile engineering. I know I had surprised him. He was silent for so long that I thought he would refuse. He patted me and told me to think it over. He said he did not know if girls would find such an education useful. We did not discuss it again.

A week later Bilkis Bua came into my room. I had a room to myself now as the eldest child at home. From her expression I knew it was something serious. She sat on the bed near me, held my hand in hers and spoke in an agitated tone.

"What is this you want to study Musarrat? Your father says it is about cars and buses. He says he knows no girl who has such an education, there is not such education available nearby and you will have to go to Pune. But, he says he has promised to allow you and he will allow you!"

I was so relieved that I embraced her with a shout of joy. Her tone became grave, almost sad,

> "Musarrat, I know you think I disapprove of all that you wish to do. I have always wanted to protect you from own willful self. I do so again today. I have come to remind you that there are restrictions on all our freedoms, daughter. Restrictions born of both past convention and experience. If we break out of these then we are quite alone. We have to find a new road and face the consequences alone. You father is a good man, compassionate and generous but he will not be there always

to help you out of predicaments and problems. Men like him are rare even in our family. I urge you to think about the choice you have made. As it is you are tall like a giraffe then it will be next to impossible to find a suitable groom for you."

She kissed my cheek and patted my head.

"I will find a way to stand on my own Bua, I promise you I will and in doing so I bring no disgrace to the family." I said this as though I had rehearsed the line in my mind a thousand times, yet I had never thought about it. It sounded so self-assured and calm. Such is the confidence born of youthful inexperience.

The next day Amira Bua came to my room. She sat on the bed and hugged me tight, as though I was leaving the very moment. She said nothing. Her manner suggested that my decision had been discussed by the women of the house. I had heard nothing of it so it must be in a secret conference. My sisters knew nothing of the conference either. Amira Bua produced a thick gold chain with a locket and tied it around my neck. She leaned over and said in a soft voice. "Go Musarrat go!" I looked at her with surprise and delight. I hugged her so hard that she whispered that she could not breathe. Into this locket I put the signed declaration against oppression and wore it always!

My mother began visiting my room every night before bedtime. She would sit quietly by, hold my hand, and pat my brow. She left only after I fell asleep.

The news of my impending departure to an engineering college in Pune spread like wildfire, first among my relatives and then in the village. People arrived to look at me just as they had come to look at the ambassador car.

I cannot say that Bua's warnings were unnecessary. The years that followed my entry into engineering college, as one among ten girls and the only Muslim girl, were not easy. Nor was living away from home in a hostel easy for me. I had never spent a single night away from family and home till then.

Many a night I cried myself to bed on an empty stomach because the hostel food was inedible and the studies very difficult.

I struggled with English, the medium of instruction. I could read it but barely spoke. It was only my competence in mathematics that held me together. Every month I got letters from father and Bua. Father constantly urged me not to forget Urdu and Bua sent messages about reading the Quaran she packed into my bag. Haider had become a doctor in a Bombay hospital. He visited me often and was shocked by my slimness. Shakeel joined father's law practice. My sisters were inching towards high school. A telephone was installed in our home, and I spoke to them on weekends. I never told them that I had not unpacked the Quaran, never used the dupattas or read a word of Urdu since leaving home. I did not tell them that one year I failed in a subject and appeared over again for the exam. Every year that I passed the exams and lived away from home was a marvel of self-discovery for me. After four such years I may have grown more confident and capable for I was soon selected for job in a public sector transport corporation. It was one among three job offers I received, all from the public sector. At every interview on college campus, they asked me why I had chosen automobile engineering. I gave them the same answer. "Because it gave me pleasure to study it, and I felt that my gender should not stand in the way of that pleasure."

I was told that there was a policy to encourage women engineer representation in the public sector. Generally, computer science engineers got the most job offers. And all of them got jobs in the big cities like Pune or Bombay or Delhi and Chennai. As a rule, my male classmates got many more job offers than the girls. All the girls found it hard to get anything they could accept. Girls had to worry about how and where they would live. Luckily the transport corporation job I got was located in Pune and I accepted it without telling my family. Up to then my visits to the village had been short. After accepting the job, I asked for three months' time before I would join. They agreed readily.

And so it was that I returned to village with a college degree and a job. After that life was a blur for a few months. Some time was spent in convincing father that I needed to continue living in Pune so as to work there.

He was disturbed beyond expectation. To say little of the women in the house who were alarmed. There was talk of marriage first then job. I refused and told father that I would lose reputation by accepting the job and not showing up. That was the one reason I had accepted a job without telling anyone at home, I had anticipated their reaction. Father drove me to Pune found a place to stay, he had misgivings, did not like the flat or the location and we drove back. I called the corporation and informed them about my troubles. To my utter amazement the head of the automobile maintenance department called me and then spoke to father. He gave him a personal reassurance that a guest house for senior working women that was associated with the corporation would accommodate me. And so it was that we returned to Pune midst deep misgivings of all at home.

I spent a year in the new job. It went by in a blue streak of learning new things and knowing new people. I sent money to Bilkis Bua for the women of the household, every month. She snatched the phone from father who called me every week and she protested about the money. I sent it anyway. I met many young women who lived and worked in Pune, some lived alone. They had an income that could support a happy life of freedom, entertainment, and friendship with the opposite sex. The promise to Bilkis Bua held be back and fear that my actions would reverberate on all my sisters and cousins who wanted to study. It was an invisible cage that curtailed my freedom, an imperceptible hesitation shadowed me though those months. The only concession I made to city life was that I stopped praying, did not cover my head with a dupatta and I drove a new scooter to work.

The next time I visited the village I was married off in something of an ambush. Apparently, father had found a suitable family in Pune through his newfound political connections. It was the first time a marriage was arranged thus outside the wide family connections in Ahmednagar. The boy was also an engineer and my father thought we could support each other's career while his parents looked after the home and hearth. He was convinced that he had arrived at the best solution for me. Absolutely nothing I said could change his mind. The boy was summoned for a meeting.

He was tall, handsome, and personable. He spoke much of women's employment. He spoke eloquently about Islam and rights of women. No boy in Ahmednagar let alone my village could speak like that. He said all the right things so that I could not find a single point of objections. His parents did not speak at all, and the meeting ended.

I wept all night on the eve of the nikah and did not talk to anyone at home. That the women of the house did not share my dread and misery, they were merry, they made my loneliness more profound. In my imagination I was carrying a torch for them into a new dawn, yet they showed no mercy. My alienation was complete I turned into a rock. The deed was done, and I arrived in Pune a married woman. Married to a man I hardly knew.

Imran, my husband turned out to be a strange, complicated, brutal man. I realised that on the first night when my humiliation was complete. During the day he told me many things that were contrary to his Islamic erudition and eloquence in the presence of my parents, in my home. His mother spoke a lot too. They wanted me to know that no concession was to be granted to me because I was a working woman. I would have to cook before I left for work every day. I was to hand my salary over every month to my husband.

And thus, I lived a life of utter desolation for two years. Saying nothing to my parents, visiting them rarely. Father visited me whenever he was in Pune for work, political meetings and otherwise, my brothers too. I said nothing to anyone.

My silent aloofness affected everyone at home in the village. They looked anxious around me but dare not ask me anything. That gave me some perverse satisfaction.

Work was refuge and recognition at work was my only solace. At work I escaped all misery, so I began to take on more and more responsibility.

Imran was not doing as well at his job even though he was pampered at home. All his needs were taken care of, yet he complained incessantly. Most of all he complained about my cooking. One moment he was normal the next a raging bull. He found it difficult to keep any job. He shifted jobs, from one to another and then was without one for a few months. At home all day he began suspecting my long hours at work. It was difficult to reassure him. Then he began attacking me verbally and physically. I bore it all in silence.

I found that I was pregnant to my horror. All the celebrations in both the homes were just so much noise and commotion. I sat through them with bruises on my body which my mother finally noticed.

I think she told my father and Bua because Bilkis Bua asked me if I was happy. I said yes and turned away. I could not cry anymore. The tears were frozen it seemed forever.

Maaz was born, his light grey eyes like fathers, looked straight into my heart. Although sad, tired, and spent I looked at him and suddenly I seemed to find a new purpose and courage. Within a few months I spoke to a lady lawyer, and she told me what number to call and what to do in case I was physically abused again. Over the next few months, we were able to build enough evidence to file for a divorce.

At that point, on the verse of filing for divorce, I called father for the first time after many months. I had not called him or anyone else for two years. There was an eager acknowledgement of my call, everyone came to talk to me. Finally, the phone was back with father, and I informed him about my decision.

A stunned silence followed, and the phone was cut off. Then they called back and everyone at home took turns at convincing me that I was acting in haste. Two years of misery and one year of physical abuse was not enough reason it appeared. Or perhaps it was, and they were dumbfounded and befuddled. They did not know what to say or do. No one in the family had ever taken or given a divorce. My father had seen enough of the world to know that it happened, and it had consequences for the girl's family, for the divorced woman and her children.

I went ahead with my decision and the consequences were sometimes cataclysmic and sometimes melodramatic. It was next to impossible to find a suitable flat where the landlord was willing to rent to a divorced Muslim woman with a child. I went from one poky flat to another but sometimes outright and sometimes later when it was closer to an agreement, flat owners would inform me that they did not want to go ahead with the agreement. It was 1998 and the communal atmosphere was so vitiated that even a reference letter of high praise, from my boss could not help me. How I longed for the safety and comfort of my village, of my sprawling home that had been an anchorage. It was a place of vast open spaces, generosity, graciousness, large rooms full of sunshine, togetherness, peace, and joy. For many years a Hindu widowed lady from our village had lived in our outhouse, till her sons were shamed into fetching her. No questions were ever asked by any of us, and my mother sent food for her every day. She joined all the women of our house for a chat in the afternoon, she would cook special daal, and vegetable dishes for us. She would be part of every festival so would all the others. I remembered all the Hindu friends of my school days who ate food from by lunch box sometimes without asking me. What had I lost in coming to the wretched city? I remembered Bilkis Bua's words of caution again and again.

Why had my family abandoned me? What was this filial love that nurtured me, allow me freedom, made it possible for me to travel this far away from home and then let me drown in this swamp of hostility, alone? I was 26 years old, too old to run to mother and past crying to sleep like I had in my college days. If I could have cried again it may have eased the agony within.

Eventually, friends from workplace helped me to rent a flat close to work, at a safe distance from my husband and his family. My ex-husband had now employed goons to threaten me. He was, on some occasions melodramatic and on others he went on a vendetta mission. He called up all the male members of my family and told them that he was disgraced, and he would take revenge. That made my daily life and commute to work perilous. My lawyer advised me to inform the police and I did that with Maaz strapped to my body.

Throughout this period, I received no help from my family, except from my brother Haider. Haider was his own man now. A well-regarded doctor in Bombay he had little time to spare but he gave me his shoulder and his strength through the months that followed. My sisters, aunts, and mother dare not contradict my father who had decided that he had lost face in the public life he now led. Father was the humiliated party; he was the wounded party; he was the epicenter of his world now. He was offended by me, by my husband and his family. He fell grievously ill because of us and used even that to emotionally blackmail me. I began to think that public life had coarsened him, that in seeking to represent his community he had lost himself, his freedom of thought. He was projecting the lowest common factor of that community, the need to control its women. It was this loss of his own faculty for rational thought that had led him into the trap laid by my husband and his family. They were not from our village or from the district but came through the political associates he had made more recently. They belonged to the city. That made it difficult for conventional social pressures to work on them and restraint them from violent impulses. It made divorce more grim than usual. I am grateful only for the fact that Maaz was too little to know what happened. I am still glad he does not know what happened during those years. I will never tell him.

And so, it was I came to be a single working mother in a lonely flat, in an alien city. Buoyed by professional life alone I trudged along. Maaz went to a day care center. One day, a year after I began living by myself, the Managing Director called me into his office.

"I want to talk to you about your personal life, if you will permit me." he said. My hands trembled as I sat facing him, bracing myself for whatever would follow, I looked at him.

"I heard about your personal troubles only yesterday and I am intrigued by two things one, that you faced so much alone, I had no idea whatsoever and second, that you did not let anything effect your work. Your colleagues respect you and your juniors adore you, the workers in the transport maintenance department tell me that you are their go to person for all technical problems. You have been with us for barely four years, but they cannot do without you. They told me this when your immediate boss recommended your promotion." He showed me a petition signed by ninety mechanics in the department. I stared at the paper he placed in front of me, but I saw nothing. Tears filled my eyes and waves of relief swept over me leaving me speechless. I had feared some humiliation would follow a discussion of my personal life.

After a while he cleared his throat to draw my attention. I had sat silent for so long. I looked up and he continued "How do you suggest we deal with your promotion". Thereafter he proceeded to give me multiple options about responsibility and location in the organisations and asked me to choose.

I asked him for time to think and he laughingly told me to take as much time but requested me to tell him within two weeks. As I rose to leave assuming that the meeting was over, he stopped me.

"I want to know why the workers respect you so, what have you promised them," he asked with a smile. I thought over it for awhile and said "I am not aware of any promise Sir, I have no idea why they wrote and signed this. I work with them shoulder to shoulder. I eat with them whenever I feel like it and I know them all by first name. I treat them just as I treat anyone else. You see Sir, many of my own cousins are mechanics. I do notice now that you ask, that what I do is uncommon here."

He led me to the door when I had asked for permission to leave. At the door he asked me never to hesitate to ask for help, from him directly if need be.

That was ten years ago.

I am now Ms. M. Pathan, Department Head. Amira Bua lives with us now, that is with me, and my son. She came soon after father passed away and brought his Urdu books to read to us. He died of a heart ailment.

He called for me a few weeks before he passed away and I returned to a grieving home after years of absence. Father lay in his bed, half his size and wasted away. His room was always lined with Urdu books, legal books, files, it was always flooded with sunlight. Now it was darkened by thick curtains. I sat in silence by his bed till he stirred. This I did every day. We talked of my job and the work I did. He seemed to enjoy the stories about my work. One day he looked at me for a long time then said, "Musarrat my dear child, forgive me. I had grappled all my youth with the dilemma of just how modern I should become. The problem became more complex when I became a father. I wanted to be modern and still be happy to live in this village. I never could tell how to arrive at just the right balance. Later, political life was like running through bramble. It did not give me time to think about anything, I could not discuss family complications dispassionately. That life unhinged me. I worried about my reputation for on it was dependent the support of Muslims in the wider area of party influence. Your husband threatened to sully your name with mine. My personal difficulties would become the problems of the party in the district. I am guilty of ruining your life and happiness. I am guilty, I am guilty...." I interrupted him.

I asked him if he would forgive me in turn for staying aloof. We wept together. I spent many days by his bedside. I told him about my promotions that had brought me almost to the top of the corporation. He would smile and I saw light in his tired grey eyes.

"Musarrat, to think it all began with that black ambassador car and I still do not know what is inside the engine!" We laughed together. I spoke to him about Maaz who often sat beside him holding his hand. He passed away peacefully. I kissed him on the forehead just as he used to kiss me. And I sat by his bedside for I know not how many hours in a tidal pool of grief. A wasted decade! He was buried in the family graveyard, besides our orchard.

Bua was inconsolable, she said he was a good man crushed by his political life. She blamed it all on the relentless pressures on him. "To what use was his toil and trouble" she said, "the demons of hatred are all around us now, every day we hear of them, they talk like bigots now even in our village. One section tries to outdo the other". Haider spoke then, "Bua, let us respect his decisions. Let us remember he tried all his life and with all his might to do the right thing. That is all a good man can hope to do, that is what we must do too, the rest depends on circumstances and the will of Allah." Bilkis Bua looked at him and nodded silently.

The family sat in silent mourning and visitors arrived till the front and back yard filled up. The Quaran was read every day and incense sticks lit. I was hearing the verses after a decade, and they filled me with a strange kind of light and peace. My brothers and sisters, their children and spouses stayed under the same roof for 40 days. The house had filled up again after ages. Mother would breakdown every day telling us all how much Abba missed having us around. She held me to her breast and took to her room, held my hand till she slept every day.

A few happy memories returned as I spent time at home. I gradually felt like my old self. I was letting go of bitterness, the thick carapace I had grown for self-preservation dissolved slowly. Maaz was mesmerised by the family he had found suddenly. Bilkis Bua was now old and deaf, but she still ruled the house. She took to teaching my son the Quaran. I had not bothered with it. I told Maaz there is one God or none at all. If there is a God, he is definitely not for public display. He must be visible only in our deeds. I told him to marry anyone he chose for himself, she could be a Hindu, a Muslim or a Christian or an atheist. Maaz seemed to not care what I mean when I speak thus to him. Maybe I will explain myself to him when he is older.

Mother and Bua visit me often in Pune. I send my driver to fetch them when I miss them, but they do not like the city and stay for only two days. Many of my cousins got educated and moved to Pune. I helped them find suitable careers. So, the city is not as remote as it was when I arrived, but it is not home and perhaps never will be. My sisters are happily married to a doctor and a teacher respectively in Ahmednagar. I helped find suitable, educated boys for them. My position in the corporation in Pune helped the family in these ways.

All in all, I am satisfied with life... at least I think so. I am too much of a village girl at heart to relish commodities and markets in the city, I look with dismay at the shrinking open spaces and crowded roads. The loss of clean air bothers me. Pune is no longer the Mecca for education that brought us out of the villages in

Maharashtra to it. It's a big manufacturing and IT city. I worry about the fact that Maaz gets no open space to play. I have hired a driver to drive him to play cricket in an open ground far away, every alternate day he has a coach who trains him. A bicycle is too dangerous on the road. I have friends at the workplace, but a single woman is not welcome in all homes and families. I notice the uneasy glances of my friends when their husbands try to befriend me. The only way I can reassure them is by withdrawing from the circle.

Now and then, I am utterly lonely, and sometimes I even envy my sisters their innocent, simple joys, and contented domestic lives. Most of all, I envy them partners who are truly partners in trouble, joy, and sorrow. At such times I stay at work longer, I answer all the emails, I walk into the work shed and maintenance yard, examine the instruments for damage, greet the few workers doing over time, I do work I assigned to my juniors, I plan for the next day's work and imagine that the corporation needs me more than anyone else.

3

ANAMNESIS

"Kesaritai, my husband's mother had grown out of middle age. Not just her gait but her manner showed it. She is no longer hastening from work to home and kitchen, back to work the next morning. She is not eager to attend family events, she used to be the heart and soul of such events. She is not so eager to share an evening chat over tea with her son. But she is still a tall, slim, fair skinned, good-looking lady, she is stooping a little now. She always held herself erect so far. Her husband, my husband's father, has passed away after a long illness and all desire and pleasure seems to have ebbed out of her life. One way or another, that does not make me sorry for her.

I looked at her from my balcony upstairs as she went about the garden around the house. Trimming here, weeding there, and smelling the roses. There is a little sit out, under the Peepal tree, with a little awning by the artificial pond. The Peepal tree was planted by her husband, my father-in-law. Its branches reach out to my room and aggravate me. Her son, made the sit out for her pleasure. Only few years ago the garden was full of sunlight now it is cast in perpetual gloom because an enormous multistory tower next-door has cast a permanent shadow over it. The awning should be removed, it serves no purpose. The Peepal tree makes it all darker, it should be cut down. Presently my husband will return from his office and sit with her for a while before he comes in, to me. He has not changed that practice since he brought in his father and mother to live with us. In fact, he brought them over as soon as he had made enough money to build a large house for all. That was twenty or thirty years ago, why can't I recall? I was a working woman then and did not care very much.

Grandparents in the house turned out very well for my growing daughter. I don't remember when I began to feel annoyed by their attachment to each other. My daughter seemed more devoted to her grand mother than me.

Kesaritai and her husband had a long partnership over fifty years, they were married as teenagers. He was the dreamer, writer of stories, comic books for children and for young adults interested in science fiction. When he struck out in the 1940s the market for such books was insignificant. She stepped in to earn the daal and roti. They lived in what seems like abject poverty now. She was a working woman when such a circumstance was rare for a Brahmin lady. By evenings she helped him by sketching for his books and comics. Their comradery was complete and unaffected by circumstances of their existence in a small, two room tenement in a big city. Her husband could not do anything without her. Everyone called her heroic, talented, gracious, dignified, and beautiful. The couple was held up as an example of new, modern, rational India. The kind that the Nehruvian era dreamed of. Nehru had hoped modern India would spawn tens of thousands of such citizens. You know, her husband died a recognised and much feted writer of the region, she shared the halo. In fact, her halo was wider for she lived longer, continued writing herself.

They had one child, a son who loved them both dearly. You know Sarita, I cannot stop thinking that he loved them more than he loved me and still does. I had no proof, in these decades of my marriage to him, that he loves me best of all. I am not sure if our daughter, or his mother would come first and second.

Yet, we were high school sweethearts, he was in high school, and I was in secondary school in 1962. I think I knew, when I first saw Azad or soon after, that he was the boy for me. He was short, only a few inches above me and he was not handsome. But I am not five feet tall myself, still I was petit and pretty. He was very bright, and everyone said he would do well. I needed someone bright and sure of his place in the sun. I must confess that I was not so endowed by birth and family circumstances. I made bold to approach him and we became friends. He was such a simple boy. My billet-doux won him over. I wrote a copious one, I copied passages from famous love stories. He took me home. It seemed a chaotic home at first, things were all about the place, books, papers, pens, paint, colour pencils mostly. Both his parents were intensely busy, but they were warm and loving towards him. They took me in almost as they would a wet puppy. On many occasions Azad would cook because his parents were too busy or forgetful. On such occasions when Azad put together a meal and called his parents so lovingly to the kitchen to eat, I was confident that he was the boy for me. Many meals and many happy times were spent in that little house. Their home became a sanctuary for me. I did not feel like going back to my home after such visits. You see, my father was the man of the house, he quoted the shastras on all issues, he decided everything of importance for the family. Our house was always neat and orderly. He had a government job but gave my mother a paltry sum to manage the house. Some days he would be away for a few days, and we could breathe easy. On other days he would come home drunk some days, beat my mother and sit down to a well-cooked dinner as if nothing had happened. The beating could occur after dinner sometimes. Four of us children would listen to the pounding and sobbing all night. Mother was frail and smaller than me. The next day she would have bruises on her body but she never complained or said anything against him. Not once, in the 18 years I spent at home. If she had complained I would have embraced her, fought for her, and taken her away. I would have found a job as a shop girl or something. But she never said anything. I often imagined killing my father. I spent many nights dreaming up the method of that murder. I could not wait to get away. What I feared most was being married off to some shastra quoting man. Mercifully as the eldest, I was sent to high school and college but the atmosphere at home remained stifling and became worse. My older brother started talking rudely to mother, and no one corrected him, least of all my father. Mother soon became scared of him as well as of my father. My younger sisters were always covering, trying to stay out of sight.

What a wonderful air of freedom ran through Azad's home. I was treated like any of Azad's male friends. Women and men were treated equally and sympathetically. Friends would often drop in for tea or dinner. So much time was spent discussing new ideas in science and politics that I could only sit around dumb struck at what I had missed. I understood little but what I understood showed me that another world could existed, and it could be better. I spoke nothing about my family, and no one asked. I felt embarrassed to even mention them in such rarified company. Azad was an attentive lover; we had an unforgettable courtship. The big city gives one so much freedom and anonymity Sarita, no wonder people flock to them. We went to the other end of the city in the train, to theatres, and to the beach and no one recognised us in the crowd. I was frightened that someone would see me and tell my brothers or father. I was anxious to leave my home and Azad did as he promised to do. We were married as soon as he had a job.

But that was all a long time ago. I do not look back normally. Then you see, my daughter also grew up, found a boy very quickly, got married and went away abroad to live. And yet I was not the first woman of this family. I would never be as long as Kesaritai lived. I was fearful then, there is longevity among the woman of her family. Her mother lived till hundred and two. Would she always be the first lady of the house?

Had she been harsh on me? No, no never, if she had been, I might have learned to tiptoe around her.

I came to their home as a young daughter-in-law after a simple court wedding. Kesaritai gave me a khadi saree to wear and flowers for my hair. Shouldn't she have given me some gold so I could show my parents. They treated me the same as they had when I came as a friend of Azad. They were just the same. Should they not have made a fuss around me? After all a daughter-in-law is much higher in hierarchy that a mere friend. I felt I was just a bindweed that grew among them. They went about their writing and sketching, and Azad went about his work. He had done brilliantly in his engineering college and had a respectable job. Kesaritai suggested that I persist in my education which was interrupted by marriage. Everyone agreed that it would be best for me, and I could not disagree. We had moved to Pune, Azad insisted that his parents move too. He could not bear to be separated from them. They bought a house far away from the city center and lived separately. I joined university and enjoyed it. I persisted for ten years, long enough to complete a doctorate if only to step ahead of Kesaritai into the limelight.

A big family celebration was organised when I got my doctorate. Azad called his friends, and I called the two university friends I had made. I was the first person to get a doctorate in the family. Sarita, do you remember that party? That day, I noticed everyone wished me quickly, heartily, but they wanted to talk with Kesaritai and her husband. The couple's charm was inimitable. Should they not have retired and let me be the queen of that one night. But Azad would not let them go anywhere. My daughter stuck to them like bine as well. I ask you, where do these charismatic people get their illumination from? People hover around them like moth.

Azad took me on European holiday to celebrate. It was blissful except that our daughter was continually seeking his attention and he enjoyed her company, he told me he wished he had more time to spend with our daughter. It was on the trip that he told me he was proud of me but only once. He had risen rapidly in the company and would be in line to the CEO. He said that he was happy he had enough money now to build a big house and get his parents to move in with us permanently.

We are an affluent family now. We have many servants and cars; we go on holidays. Kesaritai would never have seen such luxury in her life if it was not for my husband. Yet she never showed any appreciation for what his money could buy. I have never felt the scarcity of money since I married Azad, he took good care of me, and I am very pleased about that. Nevertheless, I worry about money every so often. I was worried that Azads father long illness would make us bankrupt. Azad had laughed off my fears. It may be because my mother's ghost haunts me. She died a wretched, emaciated, ailing woman when she was barely fifty. I could not see her before she died but I went for the funeral and did not talk to my father or brother. They are nothing to me. I talk to my sisters sometimes. I do not visit my family members at all, we have nothing in common really. Sarita, my friend, you have no idea what it means to have no family to hold on to, to feel beholden to another family.

I could not find a fault with Azad if I wanted, and I did not want to. He had given me much from the time we met. I only wish I did not have to share him with anyone. I found a job as a social worker in a large NGO dedicated to helping women in distress. I wrote long reports on the number of widows we saved, child marriages we prevented, sexual harassment and domestic violence cases we took up. I tried to rise up in the hierarchy so that I could hold my own in this household of illustrious people. Political parties turn to me for reports on women's issues. Of course, I believed in the mission you know that! Even that seems a long time ago now, but it was not so long ago, was it?

Kesaritai had been a widow for ten years, alone and a shadow of her former self now. I snap at her and say mean things to her. It gives me some relief; I cannot tell you why. At first, she looked startled, stared at me for a long time as though she was seeing me for the first time, then she shrugged and ignored my bad tempers.

This infuriated me. I took to disconcerting her in front of visitors. She had more visitors than I did even when she was a widow. Visitors looked embarrassed but she did not react. Of course, I am no fool. I said nothing when her son was around.

I knew Azad would never doubt me if someone else told him I was rude to his mother. We had been together too long for that. I waited for Kesaritai to tell him about my rudeness, but she did not, or so it appeared. Don't you think Azad would have asked me if she had complained to him? So, I did it more frequently and then everyday as soon as Azad was out of the house. Kesaritai did not respond, she busied herself with books and newspapers and visited her friends if she felt like it. She began to watch TV shows as well. Relatives and friends visited her and brought gifts of fruit and sweets, she received them with pleasure. Kept them in her room and ate them when she pleased. With Azad around there was a limit to what I could say or do to her.

How dare she ignore me? I lay in bed thinking of her insolence but there was nothing I could do. This aggravated me intolerably for ten long years. Then after she turned eighty her medical expenses began rising, but her son was ever solicitous. He thought nothing of hiring a full-time nurse for his mother. The nurse was always around, and I had to keep away from her or the nurse would tell Azad. They occupied the ground floor. Azad took me abroad and we visited our daughter often. Somehow my daughter and I have a glass wall between us. I tell you Sarita in confidence, I do not know how to understand it or bridge it anymore. She hardly ever visits me for long spells, she flies in and out.

Then I hit upon a way to upset Kesaritai. I told Azad we needed to renovate and paint the house. It had been too long, he agreed. I told him his mother was looking frail and would need to be shifted out to an elderly care home till the repairs lasted. He agreed. He said it that it was only a rational decision till the repairs were finished. She should be comfortable. Then he broke the news to his mother. Kesaritai looked alarmed, sad, and confused. I cannot tell you how much pleasure that moment gave me. But it was only a moment. She did not question her son. Her belongings were packed, and Azad drove his mother and nurse away after a week. He settled her in and returned. Reassured her that it would all be done in a month. I heaved a sigh of relief. I was queen at last.

Then I took over the repair work and planned to improve the whole shebang. Money was no constraint. Azad talked of his mother sometimes. But in such a large house, with so many servants and his responsibilities at work even he forgets. One day he was beside himself. He had visited his mother and she looked disoriented. It seems she took a long time to recognize him. As time went by, he looked increasingly worried. After six months it became worse, and Azad was convinced something was ailing her. He took a trusted doctor along. The doctor told him that his mother was experiencing the onset of Alzheimer's. Kesaritai did not return to her son's house.

I don't know why I tell you all this today Sarita, I am meandering and rambling, do my words sound incoherent? It must be the sedatives. They say I have a degenerative muscular disease. Poor Azad. You are my only true friend Sarita. I was queen of this house for only ten years. They flew by. Now I am ill too and so you have come such a long way to see me. We have a new housekeeper, and she is such a terror. She rules us like a queen. We cannot do without her nowadays, you see. But I suspect she has her own agenda."

4

Abidance

Rohan woke up abruptly. He lay in bed and looked at the canescent light in the horizon through the window. It was quiet in the house. All the grown-ups were asleep from the sound of it. He stretched and stayed comfortably in bed and recalled the dream he had last night. Vivek and he had driven off on a scooter through the city. The rush of breeze was on his cheeks, ruffling his hair and he was blissfully happy. Vivek was younger but somehow, he was driving. That's because he was taller, his legs longer and he was a friendly braggart anyways. They stopped somewhere and filled the tank with petrol. They set off again. They stopped again to buy candy at that moment in the dream Rohan realised that he was using his father wallet. A moment of anxiety about the consequences followed but it was drowned out in the rush of speed and joy.

It was still quiet in the house. He looked at the wall clock by which his life was planned and measured; it was barely 5 am. He yawned and lay still.

Rohan could hear his heart beating. He visualised the heartbeat and blood flow like his teacher had told him holding out his fist and replicating the sounds of the heart. That was day before in an online class or was it yesterday? He could not remember. All the classes were the same these days. He could not see the expression on Vivek's or Arun's face when teacher described the fist size mass of muscles that kept our blood flowing. Before school had shut down, due to the outbreak of covid-19 infections, he would look at them and find them looking at him when something interesting or funny happened in class. They shared furtive glances too when something did not auger well.

Rohan thought this class teacher in grade 2 had not been kind at all, she had not allowed them to sit together in class. She had laughingly told his parents that Vivek and Arun were a tremendous source of excitement for him. She repeated it twice to his annoyance, then she said, "otherwise Rohan is a pliant student willing to please his teachers". He could remember the days of the week then because on Tuesday, Thursday, and Friday they had one hour off for sports. That was what they looked forward to most. And the time after school when they played in the school yard till their parents came to pick them up, inevitably late. Happily, for Rohan his grandfather arrived last and was usually so apologetic that he let him play a little longer on the jungle gym and swings. Vivek, Arun and he would swing upside down like Tarzan on the bars and call out to each other. All that seemed to have happened long, long ago.

Rohan shifted in bed and turned towards the window again. The light through the window was weak but the birds were up and about as thought their school never shut down. Why did birds not get corona virus? He would ask his father. His father knew all the answers. Rohan thought he was the most intelligent man in the world after his grandfather. His mother somehow did not have so many ready answers. Yet she had been to the same school and college as his father!

A gust of wind and rain came down on the trees outside. The sound of raindrops on leaves was musical, first it hit the higher leaves then the lower ones and last it fell on the bushes. In the bosk by his apartment there were many trees and bushes thick with birds. Rohan recognised the bird calls, the short persistent call, the long whistle, the sharp calls. The crow could dominate any cluster of sounds. He could see birds on the trees around his house and during the long months of seclusion he had learned to spot all the birds with a binoculur. His father told him their names. He had also learned to watch the sky and stars and planets thought the telescope his mother bought for him. His father taught him star names and locations. There was no virus to fear out there either, why did humans get it? His father did not know either.

The grownups talked about how many people had died of the virus when they were not working over their laptops. It was number he could not recognize. A phone call would make them all sad for a day. Some uncle died one day and two old aunts on another day, they had all just returned from a family wedding. Rohan felt a chill pass through his body with all this talk of that ugly virus. Oftentimes the sky was not clear enough to see the stars. These monsoon days compounding his lonesomeness. The road outside was pitted with potholes and covered with slush, it was not much fun to cycle on it either. Some nights he waited for clouds to clear then he would walk to the balcony where the telescope was set up. When everyone was deeply asleep, he would seek out at his happy companions by night. He would talk to Sirius and ask him how it was all up there.

He heard sounds in the kitchen below. A little later mother came to his bed side, ruffled his hair. Her hands were cool like the breeze of his dreams, it reminded him of the scooter ride. Mother said that it was 7:30 am in his ear. He should wash, have breakfast, and get ready for school. He pretended to sleep. The thought of drinking milk made him ill. Mother returned fifteen minutes later to find him in the bathroom. He arrived in the kitchen and began telling mother about his dream over breakfast. She was amused about the wallet he used. His father and grandfather joined the table on by one.

His parents took turns over who would fix breakfast. On the days it was father turn he would dash out to buy ingredients. Rohan could eat nothing after his glass of milk most weekdays. He would walk away to his room and get his books and laptop together while grandfather lamented his meagre appetite loudly. Rohan ate nothing till noon and grandfather wondered aloud how he would ever get taller and stronger. He said the same thing every morning. These days grandpa had to force him to eat even at noon. One of the adults was assigned to watch over him by turn so he did not throw the food away.

Before school shut down, the grown-ups would disappear to their offices, and he would go off to school and afterwards to a day care or to his maternal grandparents would fetch him if needed. In all these places he had friends to play with. Now, all of them were working from home. They stared at computer screens from 9 am to 7 pm. His parents, both IT engineers, worked longer hours than that on most days. Rohan knew all the jargon now, client calls and bugs that hounded his mother through the day and late into the evening. This was the first time he saw it close-up, and it made him anxious. Could some persons unknown and unseen to him command all her waking hours? He felt afraid for her and held her hand tight every night when she came to put him to bed.

Someone was hurrying father as well these days, if he was not working on his computer, he was talking on his mobile phone near the window and Rohan could hear. And grandpa, he talked about some online trading loss and profits, bottom line, and top line. Rohan had no idea what it all meant. All the grownups were a jittery lot. On the day grandpa made a lot of money, he would look very happy and once he ordered a new car in a fit of glee but most of the time, he looked nervous and make a big fuss about Rohan's poor diet.

The dreary routine continued for months on end. Schools did not open. One night as he tossed and turned, he heard a movement in his parents' room. His mother's voice was sobbing in pain. He ran into their room. She lay doubled up on the floor. She turned to him and cried out. He ran to wake up father and ran down to wake up his grandfather, "Mother is in pain she is crying, hurry up" he said.

Father always slept as if he was unconscious. After a few shakes he got up. In twenty minutes, grandpa and father carried mother into the car and drove them all to the hospital.

While he waited for what seemed like ages in the empty room outside Rohan's heart was pounding in his throat he thought. Only a nurse sat at a desk at a distance. She was also looking at a screen. Rohan sighed. Father came out and sat beside him. Held his hand tight and told him not to worry. "The doctors will look at her carefully and decide what to do. You should go home with grandpa, and I will wait here. It is nothing serious."

Rohan did not want to go but disobeying his father was something he rarely did and one look at his grandpa's face persuaded him that it was not a time to trouble them. Mother was away for 5 days. Father said they were flushing out her infected kidney.

Alone at home, one day Rohan fell asleep in his small bathtub talking to his dinky cars. They were floating around him in the tub when he last remembered. His father found him when he returned from the hospital. Grandpa had gone quite crazy looking for him, he was almost weeping. He kept saying "I looked everywhere, I called all his friends, I looked under the bed and inside each cupboard. I ran out into the bosk. I did not look inside the bathtub." Rohan was half asleep when received a scolding from father who was shouting in a soaring, excited voice as he lifted him out of the tub. The next day Rohan had a fever and a cold.

Everyone was worried that he may have got infected with covid in the hospital during a visit to see his mother. He had insisted on that visit, protested by refusing all food, he refused to accept his father's word that she was well. A man from the clinic came to test him and father and grandfather for covid. In his life of 9 years this was quite certainly the most frightening time ever or so he told his aunt Anjali when she called. Was the dreaded virus inside him now and was he going to die, would his father die and grandpa too? Maybe his mother would not die, he hoped so. His thoughts were in a constant turmoil. Grandpa reassured him continually. He became a bundle of nerves till the results came after 24 hours, they were all negative.

Mother returned from hospital, pale and worn out. The doctor told her to rest, walk, and drink water regularly. She went right back to work instead. So did father. They talked of a loan for a second home in the countryside that had to be returned. So did grandpa, he went back to trading online. The dreary routine began all over again but with a difference. Rohan was now to live his life on a tighter schedule. He had been promoted to class four and studies were harder or so his father told him. He could hardly remember what happened in class three and he was in four already! The timetable was ready, father had made it! On alternate days a teacher would teach him to play the piano online. The teacher used to come home once a week earlier. His time was marked by hours and minutes. First school, then homework, then music and only half hour at 3 pm and one hour at 6 pm for play.

He stared at father's plan pinned up on the soft board in his room and at father alternately. Father preempted the mutinous look in Rohan's eyes by saying,

"I studied more than this every day when I was your age, you can ask grandpa. That is why you live in much comfort in a large house, go to a good school. That is why we have four cars and three motor bikes but above all else we must study so that we are not ignorant like the watch man, driver, milk man and house maid. You don't want to grow up like the watch man's children who play all day, do you? They will become watch men when they grow up and live in a hovel in the basement. Besides, since you have no friends to play with these days and there is no playground in the neighbourhood where you may be safe while we work, you may as well study more mathematics and science."

"What about my book reading time, my free time?" asked Rohan angrily. Rohan cherished the book reading time. His aunt Anjali gave him books of all kinds, fairy tales that still secretly enchanted him though his friends dismissed them in favour more action-oriented fiction and TV. Specially the ugly duckling who surprises everyone, Aladin's lamp and Jack and the Bean Stalk. He loved to read and reread them. He liked animal stories too, he read White Fang three times. This summer he had read 200 stories in a fat book. On the phone, his father told his relatives very proudly that the boy can read for hours without food.

Whenever he visited Aunt Anjali before the pandemic, she would ask him what he had read, and he would describe the stories he most enjoyed. The flow of his words followed her as she pottered around. He would stand himself on a stool besides her as she cooked stopping his chatter only to ask her how she was going to cook the chicken, eggs, or dessert. Rohan talked about the stories and then other things on his mind. He talked continuously as though time would run out, but his thoughts would not. Grandpa would then say Rohan talks the most to Aunt Anjali and he eats all she gives him to eat. One day he asked her how old the sofa, carpet in her living room was. She supposed about 50 years old. "Why are not changing these things," he said. "Well, I got the sofa re-upholstered, and the carpet cleaned, it looks fine, don't you think?" she answered cheerily.

"What about your car?" he asked. "Got it serviced, it works fine," she said. Rohan had felt and looked perplexed. The thought had stayed with him, he asked her similar questions again on another visit.

"Rohan, free time is in vacations, not around the year, next year if we are rid of Covid-19 we will go to Paris." father said. Father's words brough him back to the present. Mother called them down to dinner. That put an end to further discussions about the time – table. But it irked and annoyed recurrently, but Rohan did not protest, and he did not shout out loud although he wanted to. Instead, his large eyes clouded over often. He knew he was alone and vanquished quickly in arguments with his father. Rohan had none of the bravado his boisterous classmates. A couple of hard smacks before he turned six had settled the matter. Besides, Grandpa and mother did not support him in these arguments. He found himself alone. Mother did not enforce father's rules, but she did not contradict him either.

Nobody else understood the basis of Aunt Anjali and his enduring friendship. What would he tell her now? The thought worried him.

Father checked his grades after weekly tests. They were all-most always good. Then he checked homework and gave him extra homework if he had made mistakes and even if he had not made mistakes. No back slide was possible. He did so every weekday after dinner so that on some days Rohan was finishing extra work till 10 pm. On weekends father slept till noon and mother rested as much as she could. Then they bought themselves and him gifts and new clothes online, on several festive occasions they bought more than they wanted and spent the next day trying to return them or sell them off online.

Rohan could see the watchman's children playing in the wilderness nearby. One beribboned girl and the taller boy. They would swing on the low branches and laugh aloud when they tumbled down. One day they would have an old worn-out tennis ball to toss around, on another a used and discarded badminton racket and torn shuttle cock. They played and laughed and argued all day. Their parents worked at odd jobs in Rohan's building and none of them minded the kids. The children went into the little room in the basement where the family lived, only at mealtimes and even this did not follow a timetable. Rohan looked at them a lot. He looked for signs of despondency that must follow life in a hovel, life without cars, new gadgets, and clothes. Why were they not sad?

Early one weekend morning, a year ago, when everyone was asleep, he had ventured out quietly to join the watchman's children. They recognised him and made room for him in their ball game without his asking. As the game developed Rohan saw that they ran to fetch the ball even when it was his turn to do so and were willing to do his bidding in anything he wished. He began laying out the rules and the rules favoured him more and more. The play went on for hours and continued on many weekends. Rohan went home only when his parents woke up at noon. Few months later an altercation broke out among them. The watchman's son protested the rules in a loud voice. Rohan told him to lower his voice. That lead to a high decibel argufy and scuffle, Rohan raised the cricket bat to strike the boy and the watchman's daughter pushed Rohan away so hard that he fell. The watchman came out and dragged his angry children away. The matter reached his father.

What had followed was a long, painful homily. Rohan 's father told him that he must never leave the house without adult permission. He must not play with watchmen and driver's children. When Rohan asked why he must not do so his father said that he could learn nothing worthwhile from such people but could instead learn bad manners and foul language from them. That was a grave danger. The irony of his father's lecture was not lost on Rohan who with a child's sense of fair play knew he was acting the bully with the watchman's meek kids.

The watchman had asked his children what the matter was. After he heard then through, he told them to stay away from rich people children and that put an end to the play times in the bosky forever.

The epidemic lasted what seemed forever and the next time he visited Aunt Anjali was almost a year later. Before she could ask him what he had read he ran up to her, flung his arms around her and told her about the new timetable, the onerous fact that he was now at the end of the fourth grade. She listened to it all. Little Atul stood holding Rohan's hand.

Later after dinner, six grownups of the family sat around the living room and narrated their experiences of what happened during the lock down, the house arrest, friends and relatives dead, losses in business, job losses and wage cuts during the long pandemic. Rohan's father said caustically, "The IT sector did very well and squeezed its workers for 12 hours every day." Atul's mother Geeta, who was Rohan's mother's sister said, "Work from home was a nice change in the beginning, it cut out all the morning rush, commute time, it reduced expenses on fuel, clothes, handbags, and shoes. Within three months it turned into a dreadful drag. Then it went on and on till it was difficult to tell if one was alive or dead, sane, or insane, just blue, or desperately unhappy. I became uneasily numb. I knew that when the count of dead and sick people was displayed on TV screens. In the beginning, I felt sad, sleepless and I felt terrified but then it was more deaths every day and I felt nothing. Then I stopped listening or looking at the news". There were five grunts of agreement. Rohan listened wide eyed while Atul snuggled next to him. "Great reminder" said Aunt Anjali, "about the fragility of our existence on this planet. An aide-mémoire, that we are all social animals not just family members and we are all creatures of habits. We are not as much in control as we imagine."

"What about you Rohan, how did you feel?" she asked. Rohan was startled out of his reverie. Six pairs of eyes were on him. It was rarely that such a company sought his opinion.

"I was sad all the time," he mumbled. He saw mother's eyes were resting on him now and she did not look away.

"Oh! Let's look forward to the future," Aunt Anjali said cheerily shifting the somber mood. She turned around and asked Rohan and Atul to take an imaginary microphone, stand on a table and tell her what they wanted to do in the future and what they wanted to become when they were older. Atul was only five, he felt shy, thought for a while, and said he had no idea, but he wanted to go back to school very much and be big like Rohan someday.

Rohan grabbed the mike and spoke loudly, hurriedly, "And I want to go back to school then I want to be an engineer so that I can make an even bigger, newer house and buy a Lamborghini."

"Rohan, how many houses do you need to live, you already have two! And will you throw away the Land Rover you have when you buy the Lamborghini?" Aunt Anjali pinned him down with the question. Six pairs of eyes rested on him again. Father shifted uncomfortably; mothers gaze on him did not waver.

Rohan stood still for a long time, looked at mother, put the mike to his mouth and asked in a whisper, "May I read stories instead then?"

5

Asteria

Amit returned to consciousness slowly. A bright light blinded him. He blinked and was instantly aware of an excruciating pain. A little later he felt it again in his legs. He heard a groan. Two pairs of eyes were looking down at him. He heard another groan, then a voice, a face, white caps. Where was he? The groans were coming from him he realised and the faces around him were watching him intently. The pain was coursing through his body from his legs to his arms, to his back.

"Rukmani", he called and passed out.

Twenty-four hours later he came to again. Through the cloud in his brain, he saw eyes and faces above him. Someone was calling his name. He looked in the direction and recognised Khalid.

Khalid smiled, "You are fine Amit, one dislocated shoulder and knee, a fractured leg and arm, many bruises and two deep cuts but nothing broken. A bump on your skull but by the grace of Allah nothing broken there." And added laughingly, "You will be back in front of your computer in a week."

A long silence ensued; Amit marshalled his memory. Mercifully, nothing was hurting as much today. "What happened," he asked softly.

This time a doctor spoke up, "You were in a motorcycle accident, you were driving without a helmet while very drunk. Some bystanders brought you into the hospital. We had no idea who to call until your friend here arrived looking for you."

Amit slowly recalled the time he left Khalid's house in the early hours of morning, as usual after a weekend bacchanalia. He sighed deeply.Now he remembered everything.

For three weeks thereafter Amit lay in hospital. His Bacchanal mates, office colleagues and to his chagrin, even his boss dropped in with good wishes and chatter. The boss informed him that he had contacted his parents and they were on a train, on their way. They would be with him anytime now.

This time Amit's groan seemed to come from deep within. Why on earth had his parents been contacted. They would be out of their mind with anxiety. They lived in a small-town thousands of miles away. A shaft of searing guilt passed through him. He shifted uncomfortably in the bed. The nurse made him walk 4 times a day with crutches. The arm in a sling made it difficult for him to turn in the bed. She hurried over and helped him shift to ease the soreness of his limbs.

"Thank you, sir. It is kind of you to have called them. I hope they realise it is nothing serious. Its along journey from Jammu to Pune."

After that Amit waited impatiently for the boss to leave indicating to Khalid not to leave before the boss. As soon as the room was emptier Amit beckoned Khalid and murmured to him that a cleaner should be taken to his flat directly. His parents would be disturbed by the conditions there. In a rushed account Amit told him that the kitchen and store were full of empty bottles of alcohol. His mother may not be able to read English, but his father would know what they were. His father never drank alcohol and had brought him up to believe that it was disastrous stuff. His own nervousness then exhausted Amit. Khalid placed the bowl of paya stew he had poured out at the bed side and left in a hurry.

Amit slid back into the bed and continued to groan inwardly, pretending to sleep. The next day his parents were at his bed side. Amit had trouble making eye contact. He had not heard from Khalid since. He groaned and pretended to sleep as much as he could after reassuring his parents that he was recovering well. He had persuaded the doctor and nurse to spare him the embarrassment of telling his parents how he landed up in the hospital. They had become fond of his boyish charm and polite ways. They were going to say nothing about liquor, they promised him.

His mother sat by the bed; a frail little lady, grey and wrinkled, her eyes moist. She ran her hand over his arm, his head, his legs gently and thanked God in a softly repeated murmur. His father sat at the other side and just gazed at him. He looked relieved to see such little damage. Through it all Amit shut his eyes and opened them briefly to smile wanly. At some point through the visiting hour Amit requested his parents to leave, rest and recover in the flat. He could only hope that Khalid had been as true and reliable a friend as always.

During the evening visiting hours Khalid came in and informed him that he had done his best. Filled with relief Amit relaxed and asked for a more detailed account.

"Look Amit, stop fretting I cleaned the kitchen and pantry myself. Bottles were only part of the mess. The place was dusty, garbage had not been taken out for days. I could not get a cleaner at such short notice, so I cleaned the kitchen as much as possible, but your parents arrived before I expected them to. Anyways your mother will understand that a young, working man may not keep everything shipshape."

Suddenly Amit sat upright and said, "Did you check the second bedroom?"

"No," replied Khalid.

Amit groaned and fell back into the bed. "There is a pile of empty bottles in the room," he said. By now his accident was a minor nuisance in the face of the new crisis.

Khalid could understand completely. They were both from villages, sons of humble folk. Education, engineering degrees in state funded colleges had landed them in the sunrise industry of the day- information technology. They were first in their family to move so far away from home. The first to have owned cars and motorcycles and rent large apartments in a city. The work was exciting, even excessively stimulating at times Khalid thought. He felt he was becoming obsessive about his own project at work. They worked late into the night on weekdays finding it difficult to disengage from the tasks at hand. Their wages were beyond anything their parents had ever earned. So outrageous was the difference that both Amit and Khalid had not told their parents what they truly earned, choosing instead to burn it all up in a magnificent display of liberation and pleasure. Most of their young colleagues did the same. Except the young female IT engineers. Khalid could not understand what burden weighed the girls down, but they were certainly not having as good a time as the men except one or two of them perhaps. Besides there were not many of them.

Thus, Khalid and Amit sat in silent sympathy, till the nurse came in to begin the evening routine and Khalid's mind turned to the present again.

Amit was not allowed an early discharge although he appealed. He had lost too much blood and his eyesight seemed to be affected. The doctors wanted to be doubly sure about that with more tests and an MRI. His parents arrived every day and nothing he could say would keep them away. His mother brough food she made. The food was strangely comforting, and father brought the newspaper. They said nothing about the condition of the flat or the bottles in the spare bedroom. They sat in amiable silence. None of this made Amit feel lighter but it was obvious that they had decided to ignore the uncomfortable facts.

They stayed for a month and nursed Amit back to health. When they left promising to return soon Amit saw then go with mixed feelings. That month had been quiet and peaceful, if there were constraints on his freedom there was also a clean flat and good, warm food every night. Amit had felt well enough to resume work by the end of it.

Three years later in 1996 Amit moved to another job, to one that paid even better. Headhunters had approached him, tempted him with the suggestion that if he did not feel ambitious at twenty – six he would never experience anything new. A slew of foreign companies were offering new challenging opportunities in India. At IIT they had been trained to rise to a challenge. Besides, of late he had found the atmosphere of the old office less exciting, he found it difficult to concentrate. His boss kept pestering him to learn new skills to fit into new projects that the company was getting. He was supposed to learn these new skills in his spare time. Amit tried half-heartedly and recognised that he was getting bored.

Khalid had committed himself to continuous learning, he was fond of saying "You have to keep running to stay where you are in the IT industry. The rate of change is so rapid." Amit found Khalid's motivation exhausting. They continued to be drinking friends, often spending weekends together, sometimes other friends would join them. Only nowadays Khalid skipped some weekends, kept an eye on the amount Amit drank and called off the sessions early. Amit could not protest like the others, he would just get up quietly, go home and continue drinking. He had learned long ago not to cross Khalid.

There seemed to be a girl in Khalids life. A pretty recruit had joined their office a year ago and Khalid was often helping her settle down. Amit noticed with some amusement that he was still helping her a year after her arrival.

"What is going on between Nina and you," he asked one weekend.

Khalid was still nursing his first drink. He started, blushed, and said "Nothing!"

Amit began laughing, "Khalid, you will have to keep running to stay where you are with Nina. She will take your help and go out with you, watch films, have dinners but she will never marry you!"

"Why do you think I want to marry her?" Khalids tone suggested some injury to his ego.

"Come on Khalid, we have been college friends and colleagues for years. I see the way you look at her. Let me tell you what I found out, she comes from a modest, conservative Sindhi family, they depend on her salary. They brought her up to be obedient. She will marry a boy they find for her. They will make a huge fuss over a Muslim boy." Having said so much Amit fell silent. Khalid had turned pale. Looking at him Amit realised he was thinking of the fortnight they had spent together in Faizabad, at Khalids ancestral home. Khalid had dragged him along for fear that he would sink into a lonely depression alone in the campus. Amit did not want to go to Jammu to be with his parents. That was the time when the mosque at Ayodhya was demolished by a mob, an event that Khalid and he had not tracked or anticipated. They were so busy with course work and had no political awareness like most of their classmates.

On the 6th of December 1991 they had both seen the spectacle from the roof top, it had gone on for days before that. As soon as they reached Faizabad on the 25th of November they had heard and seen nothing else but the strife. Amit learned that some people thought that a mythological God was born exactly at the spot where a mosque stood. His mother and father had told him stories about the God, but they were stories or so he had assumed once he heard them. They were too outlandish to be true! He was astounded about the conviction with which the spot of his birth was estimated and repeated. There was no scientific fact to prove the accuracy of their conviction yet here was mayhem because they were convinced. All the natural sciences and logic he had studied in school could not explain what was going on around him. Khalid and he saw hordes of men in saffron, with saffron flags and ash marks on their foreheads. Police was all around the town. They heard the news on radio every day, everyone was waiting with baited breaths about what will happen next. They heard that the mosque would be broken since it was built by a Muslim conquer Babur but there was no proof that it was indeed built by Babur just as there was no proof that the mythological hero existed. They were trapped in an environment that was thick with tension, there was talk of bloodshed and turmoil and then they saw the blood. Two of Khalids cousins were injured seriously, one passed away on the road. They went for the funeral, but they were not allowed out of the house otherwise. Khalid grandfather predicted that nothing would be the same ever again. Khalid and Amit were to recall the words many times in their lives as they observed the changing social climate.

A deep sigh brough Amit to the present. Their usual practice was companiable silence, Amit rarely broke it, it was Khalid who had the gift of articulation and assertion in their relationship. Amit was also convinced that Khalid was the clearer thinking of the two and not just a brilliant computer programmer. Khalid sighed a couple of times, said nothing, and left soon after dinner.

Amit had no idea what to do with his new, more enormous salary. He was no bon -vivant. His tastes in clothes, food and personal accessories could not consume his income. He decked his flat simply, elegantly, tastefully in a style he had admired long ago. He bought books by authors he had heard about, he shelved them and tried to read them whenever his hectic work schedules allowed him. He bought an apartment on a mortgage to force himself to save and realised he was behaving exactly like his parents wanted him to. He thought of sending some money to his parents than decided against encouraging a new dependency. He did not look forward to their visits either. He was restless and uneasy throughout their stay because he could not be himself. Of late he was fobbing them off with promises of visiting them instead.

He thought of offering some money to Khalid. He noticed that his friend was often broke these days. He supposed dates with Nina were expensive. Khalid brushed off the offer of money brusquely. Their drinking dates continued but Khalid insisted on moderation and sometimes abstinence. Of late he was often away, at home with his parents. Amit was forced into the company of other friends Aman, Dara and Rajan none of whom bothered with moderation on weekends.

One day Khalid dropped by, he was particularly gloomy. He refused a drink. Sat down with some lime juice instead as Amit poured out a drink for himself. When he spoke finally, he told Amit that his parents would never accept Nina. They were frantic because his sister Saba who was also an IT engineer wanted to marry a boy of her own choice. His mother had threatened to kill herself if she refused to marry a cousin instead. Apparently, the marriage was arranged long ago without Saba's consent. He described the uproar in their home. The stress had caused him to minimize his visits home till his father got a stroke and had to be nursed for months. Now he felt responsible as the eldest son. He was sending money home every month. As he stopped speaking Khalid seemed resigned, as thought he had decided what to do. Amit was astounded at the quagmire, upset that he was not told earlier. He knew Saba. She was their junior in college, she entered the year they graduated. Khalid had tutored her himself for the entrance exam. He knew just how competent she was. He could not imagine her tied down to a cousin just because her mother had thought it fit. He looked at Khalid for a long time. There were dark circles under his eyes, he had grown thinner. No wonder he was so much more frugal these days. Amit admired his asperity, clarity of his thought process. He had confronted a life altering situation and decided how to meet it. In his place Amit knew he would be struggling, undecided and confused. Khalid had held on to the old job and was promoted in quick rounds. He had broken off from Nina, he said he felt nothing but relief. At least that was going well for him.

"I never imagined I would feel so alienated from the parents who nurtured me, I have nothing in common with them anymore. It is only 10 years since I left home for IIT, but it seems an eternity. They seem frozen in another world. Going around in a tight orbit forever. In fact, I fear they have retreated into a smaller orbit since the mosque fell. They seem to think the education we have acquired is incidental. It was only a tool to get a good job, security. They think that life, customs, traditions should carry even more fervently than before. They constantly present examples of other children who did not disappoint their parents." Khalid spoke in a dreary tone as though to himself.

Amit agreed quickly and vigorously, "Khalid, you take yourself home whenever they need you. I cannot bring myself to go home for more than a few days, sporadically. I am always making excuses to stay away. There is nothing to do at home except to eat meals, greet some relatives who come calling. They ask you the same questions and then they ask you about marriage plans. As though all our lives were a plan, from schools, to college, to work and marriage and children and their school in never ending cycles. The planner is always someone else it appears. They have no new ideas or topics of conversation."

A long silence followed this surge of frustration.

Khalid sighed, "Amit, we will be old one day and our world view may seem narrow to the next generation. What should one do? Reject it all, break them off, these strings that keep us harnessed to families. Or should we accept the constraints and then try persuasion. I do not know what it would be like to have no family, nothing to hold you back, no roots, no belonging to a clan, no identity. I am too frightened to find out how it feels myself. Saba is ready to try it. She has not come home in a year and has no intention of doing so. She does not talk to anyone except me. And it is not as if she has found a suitable boy for herself. She is simply happy to be free, independent, self-sufficient."

Amit endorsed Saba's audacity by thumping the table, "May the force be with her." Khalid's brooding was interrupted, he turned to look at Amit.

"What about you Amit, have you found someone again?"

"Never again!" he replied without hesitating. " I saw a star and tried to hold it."

Khalid continued to stare at Amit as if he had not heard his answer. No words were spoken. Only among old friends are such silences laden with meaning.

Khalid knew everything about Rukmani. She taught French as a second language option in their college to make ends meet while she worked on her PhD in Philosophy in another university close by. She was like no other girl they had ever met or seen. She was beautiful, her large black eyes, black hair and brown skin shone with an unusual radiance. But it was her voice that captivated the listener. Low musical, clearly audible even at a distance. She wore cotton sarees with full sleeved blouses like many other women they knew but that is where the similarity ended. Everything about her was radically different, her knowledge, confidence, independent ways. Some of the Calcutta boys in their class had enough courage to talked to her. They could talk endlessly about films and books and philosophy in the cafe. They would all lapse into Bengali ever so often. These sessions would spill into the wee hours. The circle around her grew to include boys from the south eventually. She lived by herself, in a flat close by. When the boys would argue about who would drop her home at night she would laugh. She was at least five years older than them she told them. She would get onto her bicycle and cycle away whenever she wanted to.

Khalid never understood what they talked about all through his college days. He had never read those books or seen the films or heard the music they discussed. Neither had Amit. But they were both fascinated and hung around during these sessions never saying a word.

One day Amit told Khalid that he felt inferior. In his small town and extended family, he was the bright kid who got good grades, here in this big city university he was barely keeping up. If that was not bad enough all these night sessions with Rukmani and the Calcutta boys drove him to despair.

"Why is it we never heard of these things, Khalid? What are these things they jabber about all evening? I feel like a bone-head all the time."

Khalid laughed out loud, "Amit, we are bush pilots my friend. We flew out to remote places out of our comfort zone. We are almost first-generation learners. In our families we are the first ever to see the face of a university. For these Calcutta gangs, they have been at it for eight generations if not more. That gives them an immeasurable advantage. If it gives you any comfort then let me tell you that none of them can match you in earnestness or physical strength, height or good looks."

It gave Amit no comfort. Rukmani did not even look at him. He opted for French as an add on language course while Khalid stuck with familiar Urdu. When he should have focused on his course work, Amit took to watching films that the Calcutta gang talked about, he began with Satyajit Ray and went on to French films. Then he tried to read the books they talked about, but he never seemed to have enough hours in the week. College work took up so much of his time. He could not afford to fail the class.

Khalid seemed to accept his location at the margin of Rukmani's fan club more easily. He admired her beauty form a distance. He worked only at his grades and managed them well. As for Amit, he offered to buy grocery for Rukmani, take her to the hospital when she was ill with typhoid, he could drive a car, he visited her in the hospital every day, he cleaned her flat before she returned from hospital and admired the artwork, books, and dried flowers on display. Felt the texture of her carpet, upholstery, clothes and examined the array of her cutlery and crockery. Went to pick up her parents from the airport when they arrived, carried their bags, observed their polite manner, went to drop her brother and uncles off at the airport when ever needed. The family knew him now. They were all well-mannered, well – bred and surprisingly everyone spoke fluently in English. Nobody in his family could.

Khalid suspected that Rukmani knew Amit would do anything to be near her and useful to her. One day he had walked into the laboratory at an unusual time and found a group of boys laughing over a joke. From what he overheard he could make out that it was about a country boy's enslavement and adulation. He knew they were talking flippantly about Amit.

Nothing Khalid said could deter Amit from his quest for Rukmani. Exasperated one day he told Amit that she was a Marxist revolutionary, someone reliable had told him so that but he did not know what that meant. So, he found out that it meant she would be against the present government, and it was no use to Amit to get involved with these people.

We are simple, humble folk we do not understand such things he said. But Amit did not care. He said he was a Marxist too without knowing what it meant. Anyways, she grew more gorgeous by the day. She had noticed him now, knew his name, reached out to him for heavy work, in fact depended on him, all this gave Amit deep fulfilment.

And thus, Khalid gave up and the two arrived at an agreement to never discuss Rukmani again. They kept to their agreement for 4 years. They were now in the final year of graduation. By this time Amit was recognizing other Marxists, names of authors, philosophers, books, and films directors but knew nothing more. The Calcutta gang tolerated him, they recognised his usefulness to Rukmani and ignored him for the most part. Rukmani always treated him with kindness and consideration.

Whenever he went back to Jammu Amit's home seemed primitive to him. His family members seemed unsophisticated slobs. They prayed, ate, burped, spat, slurped their tea, farted without embarrassment, and snored like the farmhands they were. Most of them had not read a single book in their lifetime. They were the reason he stood no chance with Rukmani in this lifetime. He wanted to get away as soon as possible.

The final year required them to go away on internships in the industry. Amit tried to get an internship in Delhi to stay back. Khalid scolded him and told that it would ruin his career to make such decisions. They had no advantage of social connections to get ahead in the world except their own wits he said loudly. They did not talk for two days. This was the second time they had fought. Those days weighed Amit down more than Rukmani's complicated casualness.

Ultimately, he went to Bangalore as did Khalid for the internship. That is where the best opportunities were, and together they found them. He called Rukmani every day and wrote to her every week. She talked on the phone when she was free but never wrote back. He tried to tell her he loved and missed her, but she never seemed ready for such a communication.

Restless, he took a flight to Delhi one weekend just to be near her. So that he could tell her that he found his work exhilarating that he saw opportunities for himself, that he would have an exceedingly comfortable life he could share with her. He was going to surprise her. When she answered the door, she looked dismayed to see him. Amit's heart seemed to freeze. The living room was full of people he did not recognize. None of the usual Calcutta gang. A semicircle was formed around a tall, imposing man with a deep resonating voice. The man was addressing the group. A silence fell over the room as they observed his arrival. Rukmani ushered him into another room and offered him some tea. Then she left him alone for many hours, in fact most of the night till his stomach crawled with hunger. He had eaten nothing since morning. He heard voices, now raised then hushed. The discussion was long and intense it appeared. He tried to leave the room but found he was locked inside. At some point he must have drifted off to sleep.

When he woke up next morning, he was alone in the house. He found a note on the kitchen notice board addressed to him.

Dear Amit,
3 am, 23 May 1992

How sweet of you to fly down thousands of kilometers just to surprise me. Astonish me, you did!

Now it's my turn to surprise you. I am leaving. Unfortunately, I cannot say where and for how long. Something urgent has come up. We will meet again, hopefully.

Please eat the food in the fridge. I am afraid I was less than hospitable last night. Stay for as long as it pleases you and when you leave, please lock up and give the keys to Shome. You remember him, I am sure.

Yours affectionately,
Rukmini

He sat speechless for a long time, it was evening when he washed up, locked the apartment, gave the keys to Shome Bhattacharjee who was a professor of physics at their institute and left Delhi.

All attempts to call her thereafter were unanswered. The letters were in vain. Three months after the slight, when he returned to wind up the last year of college, he found out that she had finished the semester off early and resigned. Nobody knew where she had gone. He asked the Calcutta gang and each one gave a different answer, swearing that Rukmani had told him so personally. Amit could not believe he did not deserve to know. After all the years he had spent in her service. Was he that worthless a suitor? The fact was almost excruciatingly unbearable.

Looking back Amit recalled the back temper that followed him for months on end. Khalid had held him together. Till his first job led to Pune he had remained in that black and blue mood. In Pune work absorbed his attention through the day and led to exhausted, restless sleep through the night.

He enjoyed the work in the beginning. Programming was all that he had hoped for. It was heady, mentally stimulating. The rules were complex but finite. It took time and application to understand the rules then when his program works it was like magic. Its application could solve complex problems easily and the gratification he experienced was addictive. When he told the computer to do something it will do it. He only must figure out how. In physics he was supposed to figure out how the world is made up; in computer science he became the creator. He simultaneously created and experience the world he created.

Two years later he first noticed he had difficulty concentrating. A restlessness that was inexplicable began to set in. His attention span seemed to shrink. He had to be at his desk all day to finish off what would have taken him half a day earlier. He brushed it aside as a consequence of sleeplessness, visited a doctor who casually prescribed some medication for sleeping. They helped for a year during which he was troubled by attention deficiency repeatedly but less intensely.

Meanwhile his work and experience drew headhunters who wanted to take him to even greener pastures.

Three years after shifting to the foreign owned company Amit received yet another irresistible job offer, this time to go into partnership in an IT start – up. From the looks of it the scheme promised an unimaginable bonanza in returns. A foreign venture capitalist was going to fund the project. The innovation was patented in America, but its Indian execution would be done by him right here. He thought about the offer for weeks but never discussed it with anyone. The idea that he would be an owner of a business and not just a worker altered his perception. He would rise in the social hierarchy rapidly. He would never feel like a bonehead or a country cabbage again. The benefits seemed to expand in his estimation and the risk shank. He felt excited, almost drunk.

A month later he had taken the plunge. Khalid was surprised at the pace of action but happy for Amit. Nobody they knew socially was a businessman in a big city. For some months Amit's life seemed to be an endless turmoil and flurry over legal affairs, accounts, new office, colleagues, and an obligatory bonhomie with other businessmen. Khalid did not see him at all. All his free time was tied up in travel and with new people.

When they met again, six months later, Amit looked tired, almost burnt out. They shared a drink and then another. Amit's flat was unaltered. The new wealth had changed nothing except Amit's schedule. He did not talk much about the new venture except calling his new office a booby hatch and madhouse. He said that his head was spinning with the speed at which things were happening so much so that he heard voices. Maybe Goddess Laxmi was singing but she was not melodious and brought no joy to him! They shared a laugh at that and had dinner together. Shared news of friends and family and parted late at night. At the doorstep Amit reached out and hugged Khalid in a tight embrace, for a long time. Khalid felt the usual warmth but an odd nervousness in the embrace. Somehow, it was different from all their other partings and meetings.

A vision of Amit, the first time he saw him floated in front of Khalids eyes. They were at New Delhi railway station having arrived to join the university. They were both 19 years old having spent one extra year after high school preparing for entrance exams. These intensely competitive exams were much harder for country boys deprived of the right kind of trainings and tutoring classes. They had both arrived at this point in the hardest way possible with means that their family could ill afford. Their schoolteachers had encouraged them and boys from their region who had made a breakthrough provided valuable coaching. Amit's height, finely chiseled face, wide and vulnerable eyes made him stand out in the crowd on the railway station. Khalid had noticed him right away, they introduced themselves at the bus stop. A friendship had developed and endured.

Khalid exhaled, thumped Amit's back vigorously and they parted.

He did not see Amit again for three years. That was the longest period they had been apart so far. Amit was frantically busy. He had called more recently to say there were some financial difficulties in the new company. A few months later, to say he had found new financers. A month later to say that he was unwell, and the company had recommended he rest and recover.

Khalid rushed across the city to meet him then. Amit was unrecognizable. He had put on so much weight that his face had changed. It was swollen, white and blotchy. He was now admitted to a nursing home, he was also seeing a psychiatrist apparently. Amit spoke intermittently, he said the board members wanted him to do things that he did not want to do. He spoke of some voices that told him what to do and not to do. He said they spoke to him in his office and sometimes in the board meetings. None of his colleagues could understand that these were real voices with good propositions. The board members sometimes told him there was a conspiracy against Hindus in India. Amit said he knew there was a conspiracy, but he did not know who was responsible or against whom or how to save the country. He turned and asked Khalid to find a way to save the country since he was a better programmer.

Khalid sat by Amit's bed in that nursing home in stunned silence and remembered the other time he had done so many years ago. He had no idea how to begin helping Amit with this new crisis in his life. Khalid said nothing at all. Just sat holding Amit's hand. Then Amit began to sob like a child, he said Rukmani had come to visit him, but he could not recognize her. He wished she had explained why she abandoned him. Fell silent then abruptly turned around and held Kahlid in a tense embrace.

6

Patsy and Fadnavis

Patsy did not seem to be enjoying the car ride. She looked uneasy at first and dug her nails into the back seat. Then she looked out of the window at the passing sights and became restless. Tejas turned the radio on to sooth her. It made her head swing, she whimpered then threw up on the leather upholstery. His father who had been humming old Hindi movie melodies paused. He was in the driving seat of his new Mercedes. Tejas swore under his breath. They drove on till the next traffic signal and turned around. Back outside their house Patsy whimpered and squealed again but refused to get out of the very car that had frightened her so. She kept up a steady whine as though whatever little stability she had found in the first three months of her life in the new house had disappeared and everything that lay ahead was likely to be even more disconcerting. Tejas and his father took turns to coax her out, muttering sweet nothings in dulcet tones that I never heard them use before. But nothing worked. Patsy sat whining, her nails dug deeper into the leather. Finally, Tejas put his muscular, six feet tall frame into the back seat, picked her up and carried her home. She was heavy and limp with fear. That as the last car ride, she ever took.

It became a lifelong regret for Mr. Fadnavis, even more acutely felt because he could articulate the cause. It seemed to amplify other underlying, unacknowledged, unspoken disappointments. He talked about Patsy to his wife, son, and friends. Shaking his head from side to side and moaning out loud. Particularly after the second glass of whiskey.

He told me about it on more than one occasion, "So many posh people around Pune drive out in long cars with dogs looking out casually, they even look jaded sitting in the back seat. What on earth has got into Patsy. The veterinary doctor says she has motion sickness. Just my lot, I have been unlucky." Then he told me about the five-figure sum he had spent in buying a Dalmatian puppy to go with the sleek, new black car. He had done so at a time when business was poor and had been so for four years. Further, he had compromised his family tradition of purity in letting a dog come up to his door front. A bright new cage was built for the puppy in the front yard. He was even considering the procurement of meat-based dog food when the veterinary doctor told him that the breed could not survive on bhakri and kakdi? "Dalmatian puppies require protein he informed me. I am looking after the dog more than my own father ever looked after me." Whenever he said this his compact ex-boxers' body would go limp.

On some evenings after the third glass of whisky he would start all over again repeating the story to his wife who had heard it a hundred times before, he told her that he had set out to amuse himself and his son. His Tejas, his atheling, apple of his eyes, the embodiment of his aspiration. Tejas who was unable to make a go of the business consultancy he had started some years ago. Of what use was the expensive education he had given his son? Was an ill luck was stalking them? His son thought the economy was sputtering. Fadnavis shook his head in disbelief. But how could it be so? There were sleek cars on the road, playing music. Stories of successful startups stories in local newspapers and social media every day. Luxury home sales were as buoyant as before he had heard, and the beloved leader was at the helm. Not for a moment did he doubt the future, not even when the infernal wave of covid-19 virus spread across the country. He believed that the leader would find a way and do the right thing. So he sprang into action when the leader gave a call to light candles. He even he ran up and down the lane outside with his mobile phone torch on. Demonstrating his zeal to the vicinity. He banged pots and pans when he was told to do so. He commanded his wife to do so. The Chinese were conspiring to destabilize the booming Indian economy with their laboratory made virus, he told her. His friends told him so over glasses of the most expensive scotch whiskey to be found. He told his son and wife so, repeatedly. He tried to lift their spirits by rising a saffron flag in the balcony and held yet another 'havan' to mark the commencement of Ram temple construction in Ayodhya.

If she was a housewife, his wife may have supposed it all to be all true. But she had acquired a garment store many years ago. She designed dresses for weddings and festivals and persuaded the socially better off middle class to buy them. She knew that orders were slow in coming for a few years now. But she kept quiet. This little bit of advice her mother had given her as a young bride. As she bid her goodbye, mother had whispered it into her ear again, "Do not speak. Do not state your opinion specially if it contradicts your husband's opinion." When the proposal had arrived through a local match maker a year ago, mother told her that her intended groom was a self-made man of some means, he was from their own caste. He had seen her at the bus stop while she waited for the bus to school and admired her beauty, he wanted a wife with a fair face and grey eyes. He was certain to have a good many opinions and ideas. She was never to contradict any of them, or she would squander her good luck. Besides as her father added sourly, as a school drop out what worthwhile opinions would she possibly have. In the informal school for Brahmin girls she had only learned some Sanskrit and some arithmetic for a few years. Her good fortune was echoed by all the extended family as soon it became clear that the groom wanted nothing in the form of dowry. Her father, who had not held a job since she could recall, was much relieved. Her mother who struggled to run the household midst genteel poverty of the upper caste variety, was even more thankful. Frail and worn out her mother worked at various odd jobs, from the confines of home and furtively outside. All the daughters helped her. Mother had never questioned her father's decisions to while away his days in assorted hobbies. For many years he only played the flute, sometimes he was called to religious ceremonies and festivals where he received small sums of money for his labour. Later when the third daughter was born, he started teaching Sanskrit to children of other Brahmins. Payments for his labour were even more irregular. Her sisters, all four of them had clapped their hands in joyful anticipation of better times when the marriage proposal arrived through a common friend, an astrologer. Her good fortune as the eldest girl was a good augury, the other girls would marry well. As Mrs. Fadnavis she never forgot her mother's advice or her own good fortune.

One way or another, Mr. Fadnavis's chosen trade as a building contractor had enabled him to earn a decent fortune. His training for the profession did not exceed secondary schooling. His father had shown no interest in such serious considerations as future careers for any of his four sons. They would do what they pleased he announced as long as they did not expect help from him. He prepared them for no trade or professions. As the youngest of a brood of four that had gone awry, Phadnavis, was filled with resolve to help his mother and rise himself out of the obscurity and penury they had slipped into. His father's carelessness infuriated him. Such oblivion was entirely unsuitable for his superior caste. Fadnavis learned to use his caste connections, his energy and survival skills to accumulated wealth.

When his son Tejas acquired a professional degree in business management and law Mr. Fadnavis moved to a bigger city- Pune and set him up in an office to be a white collared gentleman. He then retired from his own building contractor job. When I met him, for the past decade at least he had lead life as a well-regarded astrologer. A hobby he had developed as a young man. His clients came into his home to seek their fortune, he let them in by appointment. They came in all shapes and classes. They came throughout the year. For obvious reasons he preferred the ones who came in long cars. Those usually had a better horoscope. Less unexpected misfortunes, fewer setbacks. They came usually, to match brides and grooms, to find an auspicious day for weddings, to launch their ventures or enter their new home. Their problems were easily resolved. The money was good. Some even paid in gold and silver when they were overjoyed at the horoscope he made for their grandsons, or a particular business venture succeeded. They had all come in full strength when he organised a purification 'havan' to coincide with the national purification drive against ill-gotten wealth called black money. The discourse he gave then conjured up an image of black demons being chased out of the motherland where milk and honey would flow freely hereafter. He received large boxes of cash on that occasion.

None of his careers either as a building contractor or as an astrologer had prepared him for the present market slump that affected small and medium business clients Tejas referred to. Then the pandemic struck.

Although client home visits to have their fortune told become less frequent, he let them into his house if they came highly recommended. Defying civic rules through the first wave of the pandemic only if the clients were providentially well bequeathed. He offered online services to the less fortunate, he was readily available on social media and had longer video calls with special clients trapped outside Pune during the lockdown.

His son, educated in a fancy school, at first became somewhat uncomfortable with his father's current peculiar trade but never enough to say anything aloud. The money was steady. Tejas too had learned to stay courteously silent. He devoted himself to sport, body building and television. Mrs. Fadnavis had never interfered with her husband's professional life. He was liberal enough to finance her independence and she valued it enough to work hard at the store. She kept accounts, paid workers, treated them fairly, learned to make, and accept digital payments when government policy made cash scarce. She had learned to drive a car, tint her hair and use make up artfully. She cut her hair in a fashionable bob and wore three-quarter length trousers and T- shirts while at leisure. At forty, she could have passed by her childhood locality in Nagpur, unrecognised. At times her mother could not recognised her. She even learned how to understand the new Goods and Services Tax under pressure. The new tax and dwindling business gave her restless nights but what choice did she have. She knew she was fortunate by any yardstick, none of her friends or sisters enjoyed as many freedoms as she had earned.

But Aditya's wife was a different matter altogether. Mr. and Mrs. Phadnavis had found him a suitable wife. More educated than they were and only a trifle less so than their handsome son. Mrs. Phadnavis told her friends that Hemlata was a suitable bride, fair and beautiful without any make up. She could speak English fluently while they could not. Her family was well to do but from a smaller city and likely to be less pretentious and reasonably conventional. Mr. Phadnavis did not want to be uncomfortably modern; he had discussed that one point threadbare with his wife before he settled on the match. She was accustomed to agreeing immediately and doing whatever she wanted later. One of the several virtues her husband had was an even temper, inclined to kindliness towards his kith and kin. He spoke in a gentle, soft tone till he consumed the 4th glass of whisky. After that he slept. He never raised his voice at her or the child. She did likewise.

Well, six years ago Hemlata had arrived in their home after a grand wedding in her native town of Kolhapur. Mr. Phadnavis was fond of saying that the luxurious wedding conceived and paid for by her parents was unexpected. Perhaps her parents felt that anything less would belittle his son. He said this often in Hemlata's presence.

Hemlata too was a quiet type. She observed everything in an extraordinary silence. A silence that spoke nothing, indicated nothing. I could never tell if she was happy or unhappy. Occasionally, perplexed by her silence I told myself that she was not inclined to be expressive by nature. Sometimes when she felt nobody was looking at her, I thought I saw, hints of dissatisfaction and sadness in her eyes. Nevertheless, her arrival liberated and modernised Mrs. Phadnavis even further. All the domestic chores gradually passed unto Hemlata. She served the food, cooked some of it along with the cook. A year later, a son was born and the Phadnavis household seemed to levitate in joy. At least it appeared that Mrs. Fadnavis senior was laughing a lot more, absenting herself from the house more frequently, it seemed that more guests came in and out of their home. Bottles of whiskey became crates of whiskey. More fortune seekers sought the astrologer, some even wanted him to preside over their family functions like a family guru. He went along then in a heavy gold chain with a large medallion around his neck. Dressed in pristine, white, silk dhoti, and kurta. Long cars came to fetch him. Old contacts bread new ones. Politically well-connected he had been from early days in his native city of Nagpur, his connections grew in Pune as well. Soon he was hosting meetings of some significance, it was obvious from the entourage that arrived at his doors. Hemlata watched it all impassively, as though her soul had migrated somewhere else. One seldom heard her voice, let alone an entire sentence. Tejas's business fortunes were not rising as steadily as his father's nevertheless he did not seem to care, at any rate he did not discuss them as much as he discussed cricket matches or the last marathon he had participated in. He seemed comfortable and contented.

But that was a year ago, after the second wave of covid infections hit in 2021 there seemed to be a lull in fortune seekers. Hardly anyone came to their house. I heard Mr. Phadnavis was consulting with people entirely online. Perhaps it was the repeated waves of Covid-19 that made it difficult to feel safe in gatherings, perhaps the presence of a child in the house had made him more circumspect now. Perhaps he had heard of the rising number of deaths that defied his hopes for an early end to the scourge and of making of jubilant forecasts for his clients. Maybe it was something else.

Deep into the lockdown that heralded the first wave of 2020, I had heard him let out a volley of abuse in his native tongue, so choice as to make a sailor's ear burn. He was leaning out of a balcony in his home, talking into a phone to someone who appeared to be threatening him. It was not an uncommon sight in those days to see people hanging out of their balconies. People worked from homes and leaned out of windows, galleries and sat on terraces for internet or telephone connectivity. I overheard the volley of curses and stopped in my tracks. I had never heard such language from his lips. He who was practically a local guru on his way to becoming a local saint. Tempted to eavesdrop I lingered. I think he tried to tell the caller not to pester him, that it was not his fault that his predictions had not come true. He cut the call, but the phone continued to ring. When the caller kept up the broad side, Mr. Phadnavis turned to his inner resources, raised his decibels, and I overheard another barrage of verbal abuse. These calls soon became daily events.

Looking back, I think that event marked some kind of turning point in Fadnavis family fortunes. As soon as the first wave receded, Hemlata had packed her belongings and left their house. Her brother came to fetch her. She took the child. A cloud fell over the house and deepened. I think, the senior members were at a loss about what had happened. It appeared to me that so was Tejas. They struggled to keep a brave face and gradually told the neighbourhood that Hemlata had gone to care for her ailing mother. After the first country wide drastic lockdown the air was still thick with fear and confusion, and nobody doubted their version. Tejas went around jogging and body building as usual. He had been an affectionate father and his attitude did not reveal any obvious emotional distress. He was a trifle perturbed by the standstill in his business enterprise by now. He would have liked to defend his nation in the army instead of dabbling in business law, he once mentioned. Mrs. Fadnavis, senior, went back to her shop when it was possible and bemoaned the loss of business somewhat more vocally to friends and neighbours. Her son was suffering from the same syndrome she whispered. I never heard her laugh after that. As weeks became months and the first wave was followed by a much worse second wave of infections it became more apparent that Hemlata had gone for good. After a year the child came to visit, and Patsy was acquired to fill the deep vacuum. Patsy played with the child whenever he came to visit.

It seemed that Mr. Fadnavi's astrology business was considerably scaled down, he spent many hours with Patsy. I learned that his wife's business was still earning enough to support half the workers. She toyed with the idea of closing the store, she mentioned it often to me. But her workers beseeched her not too. They would settle for lower wages they had assured her. I suspect she dreaded the prospect of being stranded in her house with two disappointed men. Mrs. Fadnavis often said, Patsy is wholesome company and preoccupation for the men.

She was right, for Patsy became the focal point of everyday family life in the Fadnavis household. Tejas took Patsy, growing rather rapidly, out for morning walks in Bermudas and red walking shoes. Running behind Patsy half the way. Mr. Phadnavis fed Patsy, took her out in the evenings but he was soon unable to keep up with her speed. He complained about her car sickness to anyone who would listen. Mrs. Fadnavis took an autorickshaw to her store every morning. None of them lost their politeness or smile as they went about life.

Many months later I learned what had happened from a friend, who knew Hemlata's family well. I understood that the beautiful, silent, impassive Hemlata found the Fadnavis family bromidic. There was no other reason for her departure. No tangible deprivation, no unmet material wants, no harassment whatsoever. No dowry had been demanded or taken. Hemlata was simply bored out of her mind, she was appalled at the absence of conversation. The lack of rationality discussions and modern ideas astonished her. Astrology in the twenty-first century! So many bizarre clients entering the house! They did not understand that the virus could not be scared away by lighting lamps or banging pots and pans!

Teja's endless TV watching dismayed her. He talked of nothing, he read nothing, his friends talked only of sports. Her mother-in-law watched maudlin TV serials till she dozed off. So lonely did Hemlata feel that she lost her voice. She found it all unbearable. Her mother-in-law had tried to draw her out. She took her to the shop and tried to involve her in the business. Hemlata had confided in her brother that the prospect of selling clothes to wealthy customers mortified her. A Master's degree in English literature had spoilt her for that kind of employment perhaps. Nevertheless, she had tried for three long years.

Hemlata's parents were surprised by her decision to leave her married home. Nobody in their family was divorced they told her. But they did support her reasons eventually even though they did it rather reluctantly. After all, they had sent her to the best schools, the boy they found was educated too, he had an MBA degree from a reputed school. They had done the best they could for their daughter. Who could have imagined the family was so strange? Her mother was often unhappy about the money they spent for the lavish wedding. The extravagance had come to nothing!

But her brother, when he heard the entire story from her, supported Hemlata's reasons without reservations. That is why we never saw her again; she was busy working in a local newspaper and bringing up her son in Kolhapur.

7

The Socialist

"You know, my father was not a Brahmin," Gopal said as he took Pinaki around and through rooms in his house exhibiting his statuaries. She looked up; a trifle surprised at this confession which oddly followed her comment admiring the new samples of his art on display. The objects on display in alto relievo, bas relievo and carved cameos were rather easily to recognize. Symbolism was not entirely substituted by abstract expressionism. She did not know much about the finer points of sculpturing. Heaving an inward sigh of relief, she had remarked rather quickly that they were well made. Most first-time visitors were taken on a tour. Gopal's wife lost only a few opportunities to inform the audiance about his achievements, foreign visits, tenures and invitations to give talks in different venues.

"My mother was a Brahmin," Gopal went on.

"Oh! That is interesting, must have been a radical thing in the 1940s." Pinaka said.

"Not really, you see in those days Pune had a sizable ginger group of nationalists who were socialists. My father was one of them. He was a carpenter by caste. My mother felt attracted to his ideology, his aura. Some of the biggest names in post-Independent India continued to call on my father. Why, our home was one of the hubs of the anti- emergency movement". explained Gopal. His wife leaned in to recount the names.

More pieces of art were pointed out, their inspiration, date of execution was clarified. Other guests joined the walk around, drinks in hand. Entrées were served by a servant on the way. Older guests hung back and chatted. When Gopal held back in modesty his wife pointed out the awards conferred on some pieces.

"Oh! I think you have seen these before, on your previous visit," Gopal said looking at Pinaka. She nodded.

He led her away into a hexagonal chamber that had figures from mythology on display. Each wall, skillfully lit, was devoted to a different civilisation. One wall was dedicated to reproduction of the Greek pantheon where Zeus held center stage, Hera, Apollo, Ares, Artemis, Demeter, Dionysus, Hermes, and Poseidon around him. Next to it was a wall of Roman Gods, another with Nordic Gods. Yet another had Amun -Ra, Osiris, Horus the Egyptian ones. Ahura- Mazda, Mithra on the Persian side. The last and longest display had the fully robed Hindu Trinity and their multiple reincarnations. Roman and Greek figures were all au naturale, clever lighting accentuating the erotic. Indian Gods, he explained, had been copied from popular representations in some temples. He said he had made all the others from sketches in museums during his travels all over the world as a student. He had kept them safe since he fancied, they had turned out rather well. He had brought them out of boxes recently to displayed them. Gopal pointed out counterparts of the Hindu pantheon in other civilisation. He held forth on how the most well developed, comprehensive and unbroken mythology had evolved in India. She was losing interest in the soliloquy; the room was uncomfortably small and airless. She wondered if it was polite to walk out and edged towards the door, just then Vishal, a young, well-known film maker walked into the chamber and looked around in astonishment at the contents and occupants. Gopal was in a daze, engrossed in his own low, well-modulated voice, gazing at Pinaki as thought in a trance, he did not even notice Vishal.

Vishal interrupted the monologue, he said "The problem is that Hindu Gods have not made it to the museum yet." Pinaka giggled more out of relief than anything understanding. A flash of irritation passed through Gopal's eyes.

"That is because we have a lived, continuous culture, we have not become pagans, heathens and kafirs in our own land." Gopal said abruptly.

"I am not a practicing Hindu or Muslim, I am a socialist" he added hastily, "but I revel in the wonder that is India."

"So do I". Vishal added laconically. He had just made a small budget, highly feted film on the neo-liberal city. Pinaki had watched it with her younger sister who had to write a college assignment on it. It left her chilled and uneasy, the discussion that followed with her sister left her even more uncomfortable. Her sister was glad that she was unnerved. "I am pleased that you have experienced something beyond your usual naval gazing," she had said. Pinaki was the acknowledged bubble- head among her siblings.

The tour ended in a well-appointed library of books on art, philosophy, mysticism, Indian socialism, and spiritualism. At that point, a few guests recognised popular Indian writing on spiritualism and the conversation drifted to the unique gift that India possessed, of multiple approaches to the atman. These exertions lasted for a half an hour till dinner was served. Conversation spontaneously returned to the material. Quality of kebabs and sea food to be found in the city versus those procured or produced by Gopal's wife were discussed in her favour. Her talent was appreciated. An elderly singer who had not spoken a word so far, added that spices and oil used by all restaurants could no longer be trusted so one needed a good wife. Pinaki looked around and wondered why these parties at Gopal's house never included young or old women artists. She had met some at exhibitions and found them fascinating. Some were bold enough to lead Bohemian lives that she almost envied. Drinks and dishes were passed around and conversation seemed to ebb.

Pinaki was happy to be excused from the conversation entirely when it resumed after dinner. Men talked of their craft and women about housekeeping. She had inherited wealth and did not have to worry about either. She noticed that Gopal could talk of nothing but himself or else his location in the world of art. He steered the conversation around to the despicable commercialisation of the art that he had to confront in present times. He no longer sought or obtained assignments where money was discussed. He did not wish to succumb to art for market. His wife hurried to remark that although they needed money just like anyone else, they would never prostrate themselves before greed and gold. Let other do it, she added brusquely. Pinaka noticed that Gopal and his rather tactless wife were well preserved but getting on in years, they were at a point when markets cease to matter. They probably had enough to live on and could afford to live away from the burse.

A bouncy, young buck, by the name of Sushil who was a well-regarded classical singer shifted in his chair. He was making his way into singing for commercials and at rich people's parties, he likely felt a little piqued at the condescending tone used by the host. He spoke up, "In present times to ignore the market is to starve. Socialism in India was not allowed to work. Now the free market has taken my generation to this point- prostrate or go hungry." After that the conversation turned to angry bickering about who caused Socialism to fail and what caused the prostration, what made housing prices surge, healthcare to become unaffordable, education to become expensive and so on. Pinaki had nothing to add to the torrent.

Gopal raised his voice and said, "Socialists are not responsible for what has happened in India, in fact they were marginalised completely." Sushil immediately demanded to know what marginalised them. There was a silence during which Gopal was forming a response. Vishal, who had been eyeing Gopal silently throughout the argument said, "Why don't you ask what the Socialists were up to in the early 1970s? What were they doing during the years preceding the declaration of national Emergency in 1975? What were they doing during the Emergency?"

He did not wait for Gopal to answer, "They were just coveting power like everyone else but with the help of the Far Right. Who benefited? The Far Right! So now we have both in India, Neo - liberalism and the Far Right", he added somewhat stridently. "I am researching a script for a film, and I can give you the names, dates of meetings between the so-called Socialists and the Far Right leaders to defeat what they knew was a Left ward swing under Mrs. Indira Gandhi. But they said they were coming together against Mrs. Gandhi's authoritarianism. They said democracy was in danger. Perhaps Gopal here can confirm the names and dates since his father s home was one such venue, according to him."

Pinaki shifted her weight from one foot to another, she did not see why she was included in this guest list. Occasionally she bought paintings and pieces of art from exhibitions for her new house, at such events she would meet some artists. That is how she ended up in these parties. She was cultivated and invited by Gopal's wife. A handwritten, personalised note on bond-paper signed by his wife would arrive and leave her no option but to accept. She looked around; she could feel the heat rising. Wives pulled and pushed chairs to distract the group, began clearing up after dinner and talking of dessert.

Gopal's wife was rather appalled to see her husband contradicted so categorically amidst his own house party. She would not be inviting Sushil or Vishal again.

But just as she thought she could deal with them two other young guests approved of Vishal's remark. Soon few older ones who had expressed interest in Hindu spirituality joined the discussion at a tangent to say that Socialism was not suitable for India. Business, wealth, and prosperity was a thing to be worshipped, it was a goddess in Hindu spirituality, it could not be disdained except at the cost of poverty, unemployment, starvation, and despair. None of the outspoken younger artists agreed with the older ones. Amjad a young, celebrated flutist born and trained in America had returned two years ago to live in Pune and join the classical music circles. His handsome face was marked by long lines of suffering, as though he had known great despair and survived. He hardly ever talked in such gatherings, but now he edged forward in his chair to speak, "Trust me I have seen the free market, known the worship of wealth and commodities. It is not pretty. You don't want to go here unless you want to lose everything that makes you human, your art and soul let alone your religion." Pinaki found not just his flute but his presence mesmerizing. He was half the reason she accepted these invitations. She looked up and stared at Amjad now. What had he seen, where did he get his conviction from, she wondered?

Everyone in the room was ignoring Gopal and his wife now it appeared. Pinaki knew that the older ones were all making money in their ventures. She bought their art. They priced their art according to the market. Those not in artistic business ventures were making money on the side, in stock markets. She knew that too. Her chartered accountant had mentioned he encouraged and helped some of these artists manage their wealth portfolio. It was the year 2007 AD and urban life was incomplete without the stock market. She had invited Sushil to sing at her parties to help him out of his predicament, he was struggling to pay rent for his apartment.

Pinaki noticed that Gopal had turned a shade of red, the colour was moving up from his neck to his bald head, he had become quiet, his fist was clenched. In the artistic lighting of his living room, the red glow on his bald head had turned purple. She observed his withdrawal thereafter. His rather well-preserved, self-image had been wounded by these brash, young upstarts today.

She looked at Gopal's wife who looked tense and agitated; it was apparent to Pinaki that she was dreading the time after the guests departed. His wife knew Gopal's ego more intimately. She was in-charge of hospitality, she procured or cooked the food and prepared the guest list. Although he got up frequently to serve drinks and savories like an equal partner he had little to do with the preparations. She organised these events regularly for him, to enhance his aura and audience. She took care to include new, young, and impressionable artists in the city along with the old familiars. Pinaki sighed inwardly, and thought, she was fortunate indeed, she needed no husband to maintain her now or ever. Pinaki was not an artist, did not have an artist's talent or ego; she did not know why she was included in Gopal's house parties. Only Gopal's wife knew. She knew that he had an artist's eye for esthetically formed women from the upper caste. He had married without considerations of caste. Or so he liked to say often. In fact, he had married carefully below his caste, well below his education and below his acknowledged stature as an artist. He did not want to repeat his father's life in full measure.

8

Disenadora

Nikky Tilak handed out her calling card with barely suppressed flourish.

It read,

-Disenadora, without a tilde above the 'n'. Designers of homes, offices, hotels, restaurants any kind of space. There were a list of phone numbers and offices including a new office address in the vicinity.

Indira looked at the card and turned a curios gaze upward, "Have you got a Spanish connection," she asked.

Nikky shook her mane of well-designed hair blond hair and beamed,

"No ! not yet. But the world is flat now she said. We take what we like from all over and make it work here in India. We can design your interior to make you feel you are in Spain or Scandinavia whatever you prefer."

Indira took in her appearance, Nikky wore tight fitting jeans from the American Raleigh Denim Workshop (or so it said on the label) and the tightly fitted flamboyant top from somewhere called the Wild Goose Boutique. Her Fendi handbag were at cross purposes with Saucony shoes that are usually for athletic activities.

Indira recognised this assemblage, strange as it seemed in this sedate, suburban neighbourhood of well to do retired folk. It was a style not uncommon among young adults in a hurry. Nikki was a young entrepreneur and a successful one at that, if her Ferrari Sergio and handbag were anything to go by.

Indira had bumped into Nikky on the road, and they got talking about the shortage of parking space in the area. She learned that Nikki and her entrepreneur husband had acquired property in the neighbourhood and intended to move in. Nikky was designing the house from scratch. That is how Indira received the calling card.

To acquire property in such a neighbourhood at the age of thirty, a property not inherited or shared with parents, grand-parent or rented like Indira's was a mark of great success by conventions of the time. It publicized their business acumen and triumph and announced that there was more where the Fendi and Ferrari came from. The neighbourhood was agog.

Over the months that followed the chance meeting Indira witnessed extended interior modeling of their home, moving around of pick-up vans with workers and material went on through the day, late into the night and for months. Pounding and banging, scraping and drills. Since civic rules did not prohibit distress to neighbourhood in Indian cities a stoic silence verging on the sullen followed the initial neighbourly curiosity over the unusually long time being taken to finish the house. Slowly an impression grew that a lot of ill-gotten money perhaps was being spent. Domestic servants and security guards exchanged notes on the flamboyant new neighbours yet to move in. Some quick estimates among neighbours put the cost of interior décor past with the cost of the property.

Beautiful old trees were cut, bougainvillea bushes in full bloom were pulled out, more exotic, plastic plants were driven in mixed and with real ones. These were placed on a fully cemented and tiled yard all around the house. That was described as landscaping by Nikky during another chance encounter. She was with her husband, a strapping young bare-knuckle kind of man introduced as Yuvi, short for Yuvraj. He seemed a lot more reserved than her. Unlike her he refrained from excessive conversation. In an odd gesture which irritated Indira he looked away indifferently as Nikki apologized for the delay. She said, electrical and plumbing fixtures from Germany and tiles from Italy took long in arriving, getting workers who excelled at these imported interiors was next to impossible in the city. She had not anticipated the shortage of skills. Yuvi hung back, looked away impatiently, disinterestedly as she chattered. But she kept on in a bubbly, high pitched, excited voice. She said the next time she would bring her children along. There seemed to be three of them from her racy account. Indira wished her well and hurried away.

On her way to work that day Indira went over the two encounters wlth Nikky that had left her perturbed. She wondered why she felt uneasy about the couple. Was it just irritation about the plot of land next doors being covered in cement. After all the city was being covered with concrete. Housing and commercial complexes sprang up on every side of every road. Open spaces, every bosky and hill side was swallowed up. One every day a new project was announced on billboards and in prlnt media. Real estate developers named their luxury apartment building Kensington Place, Palermo Point, Amalfi Hights, Milan Mansion, Casa Blanca, Syracuse Heritage, Seville House, Bilbao Dynasty, Palma Palace with some compromises like Brahma Nancy, Veda Villa and Adani Atelier Greens. But all these were faraway places in Europe, imagination, and cost. People who flocked to these new developments must exist, must see visions what Indira could not. But then she was not young anymore.

Gradually something took shape in the new house, the number of workmen rambling around diminished. What could be seen from without, the upholstery and fixtures, glass, chrome, marble, the lighting suggested somewhat bordering on unhomeliness. The house has taken the appearance of a five-star hotel an elderly man in the neighbourhood remarked. That is when Indira grasped what was peculiar about its appearance.

One afternoon, almost two years later there was an extra-ordinary amount of commotion, and it became apparent that the family had moved in with a dog.

There after Indira saw nothing of the members. They left the house and arrived in long cars with dark windows. Their servants seemed to live in with them and those that came from without arrived on motorcycles. There was a bodyguard too it appeared from his menacing look and very dark glasses.

On weekends there were frenzied parties. She heard voices, music, on a couple of occasions she saw from her balcony a big, dark silhouette appear on the terrace of that house, its arrival used to be followed by a loud noise of shattering glass. One night Indira sat up waiting for it. It was well past mid night on a hot summer night. Chronic insomnia, noise from the house and heat had kept her wide awake. The silhouette arrived, the face became clear as the cloud moved, and moon came out. It was Yuvraj, he leaned over and threw out a bag full of bottles into the concrete yard behind. They fell in a noisy crash. Moonlight lit them up flying into a million shining brecciates as they hit concrete. The brisance was followed by loud laughter from within, first a woman's then a man's voice. It seemed that the party was going rather well. It was a strange ritual, nevertheless.

It was astonishing, Indira thought, that their all-night parties did not end up in washed out faces and bloated bodies. She envied their youth. And their ability to keep their bodies so well-toned. On another occasion when they met on the road Nikky told her that a personal trainer spent a good part of the weekday mornings with them she was told on another occasion when she met Nikky. The trainer arrived at 5 am and they exercised for two hours together.

"I cannot live without Ali; my personal trainer is my lifeline." Nikky said breathlessly. "None of the clothes I love so much would ever fit me. Yuvi can manage with running and weightlifting in any old gym, but I need someone to motivate me every day and watch over my body. Count my calories and do the math. We work all day, kill ourselves so, someone ought to look after us don't you think? Ali is a trainer for top film stars, you know, that is how I found him at a party in Bombay. But Ali he was getting tired of their demands, insecurities, and diva acts, I convinced him to move to Pune, there are plenty of rich people living in Pune now you know. I set him up and told him to make time for me...."

Indira scurried away, not as fast as he would have liked to. Constraints of neighbourly graciousness, stiff legs and wooden head from insomnia slowed her down. The clothes Nikky wore, the colour of her hair, the intercontinental accent she imitated, her bounce and go, nervous energy was all so unsettling. The entire package she came in was odd. Well at least in this locality, at least so far. Was there another universe taking shape while she lay awake, Indira thought? Was not her high-pitched boss saying, 'adapt, innovate, transform or perish' at every departmental meeting. Had not so many older colleagues got the pink slip because they were too slow? It was indeed changing Indira acknowledged and with the speed of light. Ladies like Nikky would have been hard to find just fifteen years ago and now they stared out of countless advertisements, beautiful people in print and on screens. Birds of passage, odd, drifting, manufactured creatures. Rooted in wealth accumulation alone.

Nikky's children never stepped out to play with other kids. Besides children were playing less and less these days. They watched TV or played computer games; young mothers in the neighbourhood had complained to Indira. Indira made it a habit to be sociable with all her neighbours to some extent out of an old-fashioned habit and in part out of her current loneliness.

On one occasion Indira mentioned the absence of her children from the playground to Nikky. After that her children came out occasionally. At least the two older boys came out. They looked around, unsmiling, almost sullen creatures. No words, let alone sentences came out of their mouth unless someone asked them a simple, direct question and waited for the answer with patience. They avoided any conversation with adults. Midst the shrill childish chatter and play they seemed the odd boys out. It was many weeks later, walking back from work that Indira saw them playing football with other kids. That pleased her. The next time she bought a bag of sweets for them all.

Glee expressed by the children was so out of proportion to the little gift that it became a frequent occurrence. On the way back from work, every once a while, Indira would bring some small treat for all the children. She would tell the oldest to share it equally with all the children and let the youngest chose the first piece. This would result in a solemn ritual which bonded the children in a communal act. Very rarely was there an argument among them over the division. The two boys became regular figures in the commons, greeting Indira fondly. They had to be taken home forcibly by the servants, screaming, kicking, crying, and pulling hair. This episode would occur well past sunset, every day.

And so, it continued for another three years. Nikky and her husband were scarcely ever seen. Their parties continued unabashed till an ageing neighbour wrote a letter full of complaints addressed to them. Thereafter the venue of the parties shifted to their new farmhouse. Anyways the new house had become old and dull by then. They disappeared frequently on foreign trips and the children were left with nannies. None of them, two boys and a little girl went to school regularly. The nannies once told Indira that they refused to wake up when parents left the city.

The neighbourhood had settled into some sort of peace if not acceptance of the new residents. Till one night it all turned topsy turvy. Police arrived and sealed the house. Nobody had a clue what had happened till the next day.

The newspaper carried a photograph of Yuvraj and below it read some allegations of cheating and fraud involving a leading bank. The piece went on to say that some papers were forged, that loans were taken against indemnities that did not exist or were previously mortgaged. The combined loans and outstanding dues ran into many hundreds of crores. Indira's only thought was 'poor children'!

At some point both parents were being called for police questioning frequently. Follow up articles about them in business newspapers and TV was the only source of information that Indira had. Nikky seemed full of bravado on TV, spoke to the media effortlessness. Yuvraj seemed glum. TV reporters started hanging around the house making the neighbourhood uneasy. Then an old aunt arrived from Amritsar, or so Indira was told. She took the children in hand and sent them to school and generally kept an eye on them.

She could be seen taking walks in the common grounds and taking the children back home from the playground every day at sun set. They seemed happy to go back home. One day Indira heard the oldest boy ask his aunt what was cooking for dinner. She heard the aunt reply cheerfully.

As is the case in India, the police case dragged on for months. The aunt stayed. The news appeared grim. Their name appeared frequently in the press, at the very bottom of a lengthy list of bank defaulters. The amount outstanding seemed negligible compared of the people on top of that list. A case of fraud was being clinched against them. Bank managers and famous clients, business partners were being interrogated for evidence. It became apparent that Yuvraj had political connections, but his connections were out of favour with powerful people in Delhi at that point. News reporters attributed the swiftness with which they were being cornered to the 'zero tolerance for corruption' of the new dispensation in New Delhi. An incident caught live on TV convulsed the neighbourhood. Leaving from the police station Yuvraj was being hounded by media. He ignored them all, he looked annoyed then one reporter leaned forward and said, "Your father has disowned you publicly what recourse do you think you will have now?" Yuvraj leaned over and drove a fist into the reporter's face. The sound reverberated and the force send the reporter flying into a crowd of people. There was a big commotion. Nikky was seen pulling her husband away. After that Indira overheard some gossip in the neighbourhood about Yuvraj's past with an underworld gang. Pure speculation she thought.

The aunt was looking worn out, tense and edgy. Indira greeted her one evening and realised that the aunt knew her name. "The children have told me a lot about you," she exclaimed kindly.

"You look tired", Indira said.

"Oh! insomnia, my dear. When you get to my age you will know it," she replied smilingly. Indira laughed and told her insomnia was an old friend.

That turned out to be the beginning of an acquaintanceship turning into a friendship under shadow of the looming crisis. Indira was worried about the children.

The old aunt had none of the airs and manners of her niece. She reminded Indira of her own mother. She looked apprehensive because she was intensely aware of the implications of the trial underway. She told Indira that she did not believe that Yuvraj was alone in the crime. In fact, she knew that her niece was deeply involved. She was out of her mind with anxiety about the children fearing that both the parents would be in jail.

Indira asked her about the grandparents. Then the whole story came tumbling out.

Nikky Tilak was a Neelam Bhatia from Amritsar. She came from a family of what could have been described as well to do shop keepers of the city. The shops gradually lost customers and business as tastes changed, malls appeared and wholesale cheap stores appeared with glitzy imported products at cut-throat process. Not knowing how to adapt, the family fortunes turned to dust. Neelam was barely 15 years when her father was diagnosed with cancer, his medical expenses and care took away much of her mother's strength and family resources. Within a year of her father's passing her mother passed away too. Neelam's older brother inherited the shops but could make nothing of them either. He was not trained for anything else. Both the children had been indulged lovingly by their parents. They were denied nothing, and nothing was expected of them. The aunt had disapproved then but her opinion did not prevail. After the parents passed away things got much worse financially. They lived off the savings and barely managed to keep the shops open. Neelam dropped out of high school, told them she did not have time to waste. She went off to some design institute and hardly came home on vacations. She had grown into a tall, attractive young girl; she learned to dress and speak like her rich friends from big cities. She spent holidays with wealthy friends, in their homes and had a good time with their money. At some point she decided that she could become an entrepreneur, she had made enough connections. She announced this to her aunt and brother. Nobody had the authority to stop her or question her. She could throw a tantrum to frighten the Gods! She did not expect any assistance from them, she told them. They could see that she had learned to browbeat, to manipulate, to humiliate. She was barely eighteen years old. The next time they heard from her she was in Delhi. A year later in Mumbai. Then she arrived with Yuvraj and announced she would marry him.

Nobody had ever married outside caste or region before in their household. Nobody had any idea what to make of a man who did not speak any language they could understand. How could they find out more about him? They were confused and concerned. Neelam told them that he was rich, came from a politically well-connected family in Maharashtra and it was obvious that he was besotted with her. She told them Yuvraj would give her whatever she wanted, she would get him to finance her enterprise and become famously, fabulously, rich.

At her lavish wedding in Mumbai to which they were invited formally Neelam brandished her husband's wealth, she never returned to Amritsar, never called her relatives. Till that day, when the police came calling, ten years later.

As she spoke the old aunt's distress grew, she wept inconsolably, her frail from shook as she held Indira's hand. Then drained out she whispered almost to herself, "Yes, we became poor, we did not know how to survive in the new world that sprang up on us so suddenly. Then we became even poorer, I saw it happen before my eyes. But we had respect and we had honour in our society. People still remember Neelam's father with deference and affection. He was such a generous, simple, kindhearted man. He looked after me when my husband lost his job in the factory. He looked after our youngest brother who was paralyzed. He never let any of us feel alone. Oh! Whatever are we to do with this dishonour now? I can't hide it, it is all over the news. More than any other forfeiture, this stigma, this ignominy will haunt our clan forever. We were simple, respectable people, Indira you have to believe me."

9

The Way It Was

An immeasurable weight seemed to compress my spine. So heavy does it feel that I seem to shrink to the ground and crawl like an insect. I moved slowly to catch another glimpse, another aspect of the scene. How could human beings survive such foulness and filth? Packed like sardines into apartments where no sunlight or fresh air could ever reach. Everything had withered and shrunk, trees, houses, roads and bylanes. Small piles of garbage littered the narrow lanes. Laundry of various hues hung out from dark, dingy little balconies. The vast playground had disappeared. What I saw around me was so ugly it diminished me. Would anyone ever believe me if I told them that all of this used to be my playground, surrounded by tamarind, neem, peepal, fruit trees not to mention my grandmother's herbs and everyone grew some flowers. This placé was embedded with a thousand sweet and joyous memories? It was a place of enchantment and delight, of friends and tireless games. Katie had warned me not to come here looking for memories. Oh! poor, sweet Katie she must have known it would hurt me, defeat my purpose.

"You see, we lived here. This was a Pune locality called Madan Colony. There were just nine bungalows here then around a wide-open playground. Each house had a garden of its own and an outhouse for the house help. A wall ran around the colony to separate us from the hoi polloi. At the entry gate out there, was yet another little outhouse. In it lived Khan Sahib our Afghan watch man. He guarded us all children from the world without. In that little outhouse he reproduced his Afghan village. He had six daughters in the hope of a son. He did get a son but as a seventh child. He kept a flock of goats to supplement his meagre income.

But the goats could not save him from increasing hardship nor could the gifts of food and clothing that came from my grandmother's house. Grandmother would have his oldest daughter over to read the Quaran and give her a little money for the effort, it was an exercise to keep Khadija in school. Khadija was the oldest and brightest. Kaneez the third was the most beautiful. I referred to them as apa, older sisters, for they were all much older than me. As little boys we witnessed Khan sahib's irritation at the young lads who stood on the terrace of the dwelling outside the colony to catch a glimpse of Kaneez. He would swear to break their bones and they would scamper away only to reappear on another day. This vigilance was wearing Khan sahib's patience down and on two occasions I saw his capacity for red hot rage. He beat some boys up quite badly and the police came to question him. He spent a few days in the police lock up. This capacity for rage was to cost him dearly later. Somehow grandmother's position as the Principal of the Urdu Training College close by and her thoughtful kindness to Khan sahib's daughters kept them in school and two older ones even made it to college. I have no idea what happened to the rest or to his precious son or to many other people who lived here around us for that matter. Most of the residents were Parsees, there were two bungalows requisitioned by the government for their employees at various times.

On this side, out there, the Sanjana's lived. They lived by the Parsee calendar and so we knew when they would be setting out for the fire temple. Or when they would be distributing sweets. Katie was our play mate at least whenever she could get away from lessons and piano classes. She was a meek, obedient six-year-old. Unlike me she had to give an account of her time and location to her parents. In those days I believed it was tyrannical to have such parents. I thought Katie was suffering unbearably in silence doing lessons all day and pounding the piano by evening. She even developed a hunch back because of it. I kept up with her long after she left Pune. She moved to Bombay and worked as a secretary to a rich Parsee Seth after her father died. She stopped studying and playing the piano as soon as he passed away.

You see I had a grandmother and mother at home but no father. My father, a doctor, left for Canada when I was very little and never came back nor did he send for mother. Grandmother was similarly a single parent having left her spouse for irreconcilable differences to peruse her own career. Grandpa was a scholarly sort, educated in UK and taught Philosophy at Allahabad University. Mother was born in Allahabad but moved and stayed with grandmother. In Pune, mother made her way through college and a master's programme to get a college teaching job. They were busy women. They trusted me to tell them what I was up to if I wanted to tell them. So, while I was as old Katie I was far freer, at liberty to do as I pleased. Her father was not just a tyrant but an ill-tempered man, better to have no father than to have one like that I thought.

Mr. Sanjana grew roses in his yard. He pruned, watered, and talked kindly to them. You could pass by his house and overhear a loving monologue. It was never Katie or her mother he talked to like that. Every year he took them all to the rose exhibition in the Council Hall. He won many prizes for his roses, but he had to guard them for the rest of the year. He had to protect them from Khan sahib's goats who ate them and our cricket ball that landed on them. The tussles were bitter and frequent. We boys laughed off his abusive rants and diatribes, but they tormented Khan Sahib. It seemed as though the goats lived only to get an opportunity to eat Mr. Saldana's roses and their calves inherited the taste. Mr. Sanjana was not inclined to talk as respectfully or even as politely to Khan sahib as my mother and grandmother were. Mr. Sanjana was rather liberal with his abuse. Khan Sahib had to listen in silence given his subservient position in the colony. He promised to get rid of his most obstinate goat. But I suspect they were all inclined to be obstinate about the roses. Khan sahib could not have fed his family without the goats. Every Bakra Eid he sacrificed one 'most headstrong' goat and distributed the meat and later bought another. Sometimes he sold them if the flock grew too large to manage. He even gave me a pretty calf to nurture.

While Mr. Saldana crushed Khan sahib's spirits within the colony Khan sahib recovered them in in his battles outside, with

Sallu Bhai the local bootlegger. Sallu Bhai was a large man while Khan sahib was small, unusually so for an Afghan. Khan knew enough about Islam to tell Sallu Bhai, tell him time and time again, that alcohol was haram, it was against the Islamic way of life. Yet, Sallu Bhai who attended the same Friday prayers, in the same mosque, went about this business of making the illicit liquor and burying it in open grounds to ferment. He buried it just outside Madan Colony. He dared not cross the boundary wall within which Khan sahib defended Islam. Khan sahib's family of nine made it their business to guard the colony against such encroachment. Police raids would occur and Sallu Bhai would find himself in the local police station only to emerge and resume his trade. As boys we were caught up in the excitement of these events and disputes. I remember being somewhat sympathetic to Khan's goats and Sallu's compulsions.

No man lived in our house. I was looked after by an ayah called Adlin, a Konkani Christian. That is how I learned to speak the language while I learned Gujarati from the Parsee playmates. My grandmother who belonged to those parts had acquired Adlin for this special purpose and imbued her job with much respect and responsibility. Another lady Salma cooked for us, and her family of women cleaned out house and occupied the outhouse. For our safety grandmother called upon an old carpenter by the name of Dev Nath to sleep in the room outside. Dev Nath had a melancholy air about him. Rumor had it that he was the illegitimate son of the Punjabi Furniture shop owner on East Street, the largest such shop in our city. Born out of wedlock and bearing a strong resemblance to his fair skinned father he was doomed to live among the Dalits of his mother's community as an odd man out. None of whom accepted him entirely as their own. He lived a lonely life, never went to school just like the rest of his mother's clan and was employed in his father's shop eventually. He learned the trade well and became indispensable in the shop which was inherited by his half bothers. They let him be, he knew the trade better than them. He never married; the melancholy air never left him, but he grew to acquire a quiet dignity. With hindsight I realise that it was an uncanny empathy that led grandmother to requested him to guard the women of the house by night.

This elevated his position and made it possible for him to leave the Dalit colony he lived in. By day he would manage the store and by night he would sleep in the room outside. He was the kindest man I ever knew and served us loyally till grandmother died.

Khan sahib was the other man grandmother called upon. Our bungalow was surrounded by open spaces, trees, and shrubs. I had as pets a dog, a cat, hens, even a goat at some point. They lived outside the house and never inside. I would feed them, and Dev Nath would do so too. Oftentimes we would have lizards and earthworms crawling inside the house. After the monsoon began, we would have four legged visitors like frogs and on occasions a snake would wind itself along a pillar and come calling. On all such occasions the women would be terrified, someone would go running across the playground to call Khan sahib. This errand called forth some inner resources that only Khan sahib possessed. He would arrive and gravely ask to be led to the offending creature. At the door of the room where the creature was last seen Khan sahib would pause, recite a few lines from the Quaran and call out "Chale jao, chale jao, chale jao...." (Go away, go away, go away). Nonviolence was essential he said to me, we must give a chance to the creature to leave without aggressive action. After a sufficient pause he would begin looking for the creature. I do not recall any occasion when Khan sahib was called upon and failed to persuade with nonviolence. Yet, this instinct failed him often with two legged creatures and he beat up the boys who tried to catch a glimpse of Kaneez.

Kaneez grew more beautiful as she grew up. I once heard our neighbour Karanjia's son, Russi declare that she was more beautiful than Madhubala. I had never seen Madhubala, so he showed me a post card he carried in his inner pocket that had a picture of a woman with large lustrous, twinkling eyes and an enchanting smile. She bore no resemblance to Kaneez Apa, but I held my tongue. He was the oldest boy in the colony and had enough pocket money to watch as many adult Hindi films as he wanted to. He sang songs from these films as he went about. None of it was familiar to me. Kaneez's beauty outshone that of her sisters, Russi told me so. He said that all of them were film star material, but they would never see the bright lights of Bombay, never become rich because of their backward parents. The idea that Khan sahib could move out of an existence bordering on poverty took hold of my imagination. I mentioned this prospect to grandmother who had considerable influence over the Khan household. The dismay with which she treated Russi's suggestion was enough to silence me. "Huzaifa, money is never more important than dignity and honour. The girls will be educated if I can have my way, and they will find employment soon enough with education." She also told me not to spend too much time with Russi, who was by now a college drop out. I attended St. Vincents school in the neighbourhood and although no one read the rule book to me I knew that it was important to study seriously and find pleasure in inexpensive pursuits like playing cricket and football, cycling, reading. Spending money on pleasuring oneself was considered vulgar, no one at home did it. As a result, I never asked grandma for money, if I had I am sure I would have got it. There was nothing that she would deny me. Grandmother was the only earning member, her generosity and charity meant that considerable resources were directed at helping those less fortunate than us.

Life in Madan Colony went on peacefully. Two episodes however changed the course of its life. One day the police came to get Khan sahib. This time his crime was more serious. He had stabbed to death a cousin in what was eventually described as a crime of passion. But at that moment we knew nothing about the details. They arrested him and he was in jail for a long time. All I can recall of this period is that mother and grandmother sent food to his home every day, thereafter. Only three of the older girls made it through college and got some jobs. One of them Abida, not Kaneez, was wooed and married by a rich man who took her away to a life of comfort and helped her family too.

The second incident was equally dramatic. In 1969, we heard that the land our colony was built upon had been sold by the Zoroastrian trust that had leased it from Bahadur Shah Durgah. It was Inam land that they had leased. It was unclear how it could have been sold. It was bought by one Parwani, a wily Sindhi lawyer. Suddenly all the trees were being cut down, some hundred years old, grandma told me with evident distress. She was left alone when all the residents sold out for money. All open spaces were being built upon. Large apartments buildings were coming up. A constant din of breaking and making surrounded us. Parwani trapped grandmother in a volley of propositions and warnings. She found that she was no match for his ways. Decades of managing an academic institution with Parsee, Protestant and Muslim faculty and thousands of students had not prepared her for the new world of cutthroat construction enterprises. Parwani convinced grandma that it was in her family's best interest to sign over her land to him in exchange for two apartments in the building coming up. He used legal jargon, promised her the ground floor and she capitulated. She did not ask for a legal agreement trusting his word as a gentleman and lawyer. Eventually Parwani gave her only one flat on the ground floor and we moved in a few years later. Life after that was remarkably different from life before that, I now recall. The high wall around Madan colony came down, the outhouses disappeared, Khan Sahib had to relocate his family of nine plus goats. I have no memory now of where he went. Maybe Katie will recall. As the wall and Khan's sahib's protection vanished the hoi polloi merged with us. I ventured out on my bicycle frequently discovering the sights and sounds of our neighbourhood, MG Road, East Street, Moledina Road, the cantonment which was a well-preserved area from the days of the Raj. By the way, the Indian military establishment has maintained it, it is still a large, clean, neat, green, leafy zone with wide roads. Somedays I would cycle up to the war memorial, rows of graves well maintained marking martyrdom of Indians in the world wars. It was overwhelming to contemplate. What contortions the human race is capable of. So many died so far away from home for what! I would say a little prayer that the priests at school recited asking among other things for God to deliver us from evil. Amen! Making the sign of the cross over my body before leaving the place. Sometimes I would cross the bridge into other parts of the city that I had no notion existed. That is where the Marathi speaking Hindu caste people lived in clusters.

Dev Nath's part of the city, our part and the caste Hindu part were apart. Only then it became clear to me that there were many worlds that hardly intersected each other within this city. The area close to what used to be the British army's cantonment was intensely cosmopolitan. Muslims, Parsees, Jews, Christians lived together in our side of town. Not so in the other side of town where the Maharashtrian upper castes lived in a large, exclusive ghettos. On MG Road, which was the commercial zone, Jews monopolised the hosiery business, Punjabi's ran the sports shops, Muslims were saddlers, they had the leather, hardware, suitcase business. Chinese made very expensive and sought-after shoes further up. Irani Zoroastrians who were somehow considered lower than Parsee Zoroastrians in the social order owned simple bakeries and restaurants around the area. I think they came to India long after the Parsees, some as late as the early twentieth century, perhaps they were mostly peasants who were escaping poverty and persecution in Iran. All the shops would shut for siesta after 1:30 pm and open after 4 pm. Parsees were chartered accountants, bankers, dentists, doctors, and lawyers. The medical clinics on that road bore Parsee names before other communities joined them slowly. They lived around and on cantonment land in large walled and gated housed long after Madan Colony was demolished. My classmates lived around these parts too, and I found out that Juda's father owned the big hosiery store. His family would go to the synagogue every Sunday and sometimes I went with them. I remember that the predominant mode among us boys was irreverent, and it stayed with us through life. It was considered backward to be devout, fervent about religion. Grandmother and mother's friends were rarely ever Muslims. Just because we were Muslim, we did not socialise with Muslims alone, in fact, we had few Muslims friends who were as close as others. You look surprised, why? Does this seem a revolutionary notion today!

I would cycle into Empress Gardens and walk wistfully through the lovely trees. They reminded me of what we had lost in Madan Colony and yet I was too young and full of hopes for the future to dwell on what was lost. That is where every so often I bumped into Russi with his Maharashtrian girlfriend. They were often seated under a tree and Russi would jump up to embrace me like a long-lost friend when he could easily have ignored me. He once introduced me to the girl called Savitri who looked nothing like Madhubala. I guessed he was still living off his father and not gone off to Bombay to get rich like he had planned to few years ago. On another day I ran into Percy, son of Daadjee of Madan Colony. He was there with his lively and chic Catholic girlfriend. Percy did not introduce me to her but offered to introduce me to her friends instead, if I was ever looking for a girlfriend. One does not get far in life without such helpful and caring friends.

Mother, still a young, handsome woman of thirty-three or so had started teaching in Wadia college not too far away. Educated wives of wealthy Parsee also taught there, they arrived in long cars, it was considered a genteel profession, suitable for women. Grandmother retired from her job. Somehow both the retirement and living in an apartment started a downward spiral in her life. She started falling ill repeatedly. Many trips to and admissions into hospital followed. It was 1974 and inflation was soaring. It was the first time I heard mother and grandmother briefly discuss shortage of resources to keep the house going. With rising medical expenses, it was becoming next to impossible. On many occasions we paid off hospital bills in installment. Everyone knew grandmother and nobody hassled us about the bills. Only mother worried about them. Sometimes wages of servants were delayed and mother felt distressed. Grandmother's pension was unequal to inflation. She thought that mother was too young to waste her life in lonely anxiety and insisted on finding a suitable match for her. She had found my father who proved to be a disappointment I suppose, she managed to find a suitable man once again through her numerous social networks. My stepfather was a wealthy man from Goa, it was his second marriage as well. I was to stay behind with grandmother. Mother left us for her new home. I recall dropping her off at the railway station. I remember feeling rather alone on the first day of my board exams as I rushed to drop grandmother off at hospital before hurrying off for the examination center. That was the day my bicycle was robbed. Something that could never be replaced, so constrained were our circumstances.

And yet grandmother continued to live with generosity, dignity, and honour. We never talked about money, never worried about the next day or next month. We ate well, not lavishly. I went to college locally even though I longed to go off to St Xaviers in Bombay where my more ambitious friends went. I could not afford to do so, nor could I afford to take German language classes that I so wanted to. The servants never left us even when their wages were in arrears for months. Nobody just about nobody, not even I could have guessed how impoverished we were because grandmother was always giving away things she possessed. She belonged to the Servants of India Society and had been a member all her life. This was something I learned when I was in high school. It was her parents who had become enthused by the ideology of Gopal Krishna Gokhale of Pune. They spent time and resources promoting education by opening primary schools and hostels for students. They led campaigns against superstition, oppression of Dalits, tribals and women, domestic violence, alcoholism, and other social evils of the day. They ran campaigns for health and hygiene of common people. They had branches in Allahabad, Orissa and brough out a newsletter called The Hitavada in English from Nagpur. They stayed away from politics, from the Indian National Congress and its opponents alike and focused on social reform. They disagreed with political parties about the primacy of social reform over political power. My grandma talked only with scholars and wise men, they called upon her throughout her life. Nobody seemed to notice our constrained circumstances and neither did I.

That was forty years ago, I now return to the city of my birth, childhood after decades spent in a job in the bank. That job that took me all over the country and outside it. It gave me no time for memories. I rose all the way up in the profession but retired before my time. You ask me why I threw it away? Well, I did so to escape a possible compromise of dignity and honour that seemed inevitable after 2016. Besides I wanted to pursue a daydream. I wanted to travel, to visit places, to see historical monuments and write history, to dwell on the way things were. I did not want to wait, to grow too old and weary to do so. I was offered money and promotions, but they did not matter, they never did. Nothing enchants me like the past does.

I just went across to where the gardens of Madan Colony once were today to revive memories, stimulate reminiscences you know. I came away miserable. I ask you; how can one explain the gruesome maze of buildings I just saw? What has made such hideousness acceptable? What has strangled, smothered, and exterminated human existence as I knew it? Would not such a deficit of aesthetics eclipse the human heart, extinguish its soul? Who would believe me now if I told them that it was not always so? When they destroyed Madan Colony, used greed and chicanery to do so, did they know what a catastrophe would follow? An existence unbecoming for humankind!"

Huzaifa was quiet for a long time. He had been speaking for half a day if not more, it seemed he was in a state of disbelief. Then he sighed deeply, turning his large and wistful eyes towards Zain his fellow traveler, and said, "Will you join me for a trip to Mastani's grave its only sixty kilometers from Pune, in Pabal village. I have heard that the archaeological department and village panchayat have maintained it. The boundary walls are well preserved, and the courtyard is wide and clean. Baba Inamdar lights a Diya every night. Locals of all religions revere the grave. Let's go Zain, I will feel better."

10

Capriccio

Ava Irani, the third daughter of a tradesman was an extraordinarily pretty girl. Her father was a wealthy man from Bombay whose affairs took him to cities across the Western Ghats. He visited Pune frequently. As with such men of means it was not possible to identify the exact source of Mr. Shahryar Irani's considerable wealth, but it was known that he had inherited plenty, he had invested in the wholesale trades of grain, dry fruits, fresh fruits, real estate market and of late he had acquired a taste for the stock market. He commanded respect in his social circle, was known as 'seth' in the wholesale market, meaning that he was a man with capital. It was widely acknowledged that he had a keen and wide eye for means by which he could accumulate wealth, but he was not wholly unconcerned about his own reputation or that of his family. In short, he had some principles. Some notions that came from decades of religious instruction about good thoughts, good words, good deeds and of countless prayers with fire as witness. He had three daughters and two sons who were similarly instructed to be mindful of good thoughts, good words, and good deeds. Ava was the youngest of his five children and the most ardently religious.

The family's expanding wealth had not altered the way they lived over several generations. It was some sort of inherited wisdom to remain simple and pious. Some of their other ways they had carried from their peasant origins in Iran from whence they had come to the western coast of India in the early twentieth century. Some habits they acquired from the conservative wealthy upper caste locals whom they competed with in the market and only some from the Parsees of the same faith (who had long preceded them into India from Iran, accumulated much more wealth and obtained considerable western education and status). Parsees they secretly aspired to equal someday but overtly derided as being of impure blood. In the Irani version of their history in India, Parsees had arrived in India without their womenfolk and married locally. Since upper caste Hindu or Muslim women would not have them, they married the lowest castes. Later they had isolated themselves, acquired wealth and constructed a Zoroastrian orthodoxy. Claiming high ground about several aspects of the faith they forbade marriage with non-Parsees, denied temple entry rights to non-Parsees, fed their dead bodies to vultures and so on. Irani's did not. Parsees in turn thought new Irani arrivals were uncouth peasants, avoided mingling with them, let alone marrying them. And it remined so, into the twenty-first century.

Back then in the middle of the twentieth century, the typical Irani household women were largely to be seen not heard. They managed the house, cared for the children, and looked after the old at home. They were taught to read the Zend-Avesta, to believe that Ahura Mazda was everywhere and all powerful and the source of goodness and happiness, to read Gujarati and sometimes English, to write, pray frequently before the fire with heads covered in scarfs, play the piano, or violin. If they showed an aptitude, they read other books. They dressed soberly and often just like local women in sarees, some fashionable ones even wore salwar kameez (long tunics and loose pants) in the contemporary fashions. They spoke Dari at home, Gujarati which was the language of the port of their entry into India and also Marathi if they had moved into Maharashtra, the neighbouring state in search for business opportunities. Rarely ever did members their kinship group speak no local language. Men of business could ill afford to be insular. Their wives even less so. The women were groomed to be respectful, obedient wives, daughters, daughters-in-law and to derive their self-confidence from such conduct and connections only. With such an arrangement in place, the man of the house could focus on the hurly burly of a life of travel and trade without domestic anxiety or unrest. The sons likewise would be groomed in good thoughts, good deeds, good actions, and the trades. Rarely did the sons stray out of the family business into other professions. The eldest son was always first among equals. At least, that was the case till 1950s. As with all such arrangements that sharply divided responsibility the women acquired an influence over the household that was not insignificant but it subtle, artful although their lives remained deeply circumscribed by the personality and opinions of the patriarch.

Ava was brought up thus, she was groomed to be a gentle, dutiful lady. At the time this story begins, if at all a story of human advancement can begin on a day and year, Ava was seventeen. According to conventions of the day, she was ready to be married off. Her father searched in vain for a suitable groom. The choice was not wide; besides he had exhausted his social connections and himself in the search for grooms and brides for his four older children. The Iranians did not usually marry the Parsees in India. So, the choice was restricted to more recent Iranian arrivals into India. From this set there seemed nothing suitable at the moment.

As his anxiety grew Ava's father began looking below his social circle. A relative proposed the name of a young, strong, handsome man by the name of Soroush Irani who lived in Pune. The young man did not have a penny or trade to his name. His parents were dead. The older brother however was a senior officer in the British army and had been absorbed into the Indian army. He was well respected, had risen to a high rank of Major General and lived in the Pune cantonment zone. This was a rare distinction and accomplishment in the community. Shahryar Irani went to Pune to meet the family. The meeting did not go very well. The Major General was a busy man who had little time for idle speculations about Soroush's prospects. After considerable hesitation, doubt, there was a renewed search for an alternative groom that lasted three years. Ava was twenty and no suitable groom was found. Ava's father decided to go ahead and seal the matter with Soroush Irani. In the interlude Shahryar's reluctance was almost certainly perceived by Soroush's family.

In accord with the preference of the groom the engagement was a simple, traditional Nam Padvun ceremony, Ava's name was changed, silver coins were exchanged and at her home and the groom's brother's home surrounded by relatives from both sides. Her father however organised a grand feast afterwards in his own palatial house with at least a hundred dishes, thousands of guests, an orchestra, dancing, and foreign whiskey to celebrate the occasion. This feast outdid all the previous feasts he had ever organised. Like most of his other actions it was planned. He had intended to make an impression of his considerable wealth and generosity. He would not admit it then, but he was also trying to overcome his own remorse in marrying off his youngest to a poor man. The groom was awed, somewhat astonished and perhaps even a trifle humbled. It did not go down well at all with Soroush Irani's oldest sister, a spinster, and the ruling force in their household. Two decades ago, Roxana Irani had put her own life on hold to look after her young brothers. She was an English teacher at a reputed school St Mary, in Pune. An accomplished piano player: she was involved with an acting and drama school in which she taught on the side. An independent woman, with her own however, small means and strong opinions was an unusual, rare entity. Nobody in Ava's family knew how to deal with her, least of all the men. Ava's mother was the first to realised that Roxana was offended, she made some hasty attempts to mollify her, "This will be the last wedding in our family, my husband dotes on Ava, he would not have it any other way...."

To which Roxana replied curtly "That is an utterly egotistical approach. It goes completely against our wishes, particularly those of my brother who has no means to reciprocate or reproduce such extravagance."

Ava's mother rushed to apologize for the offence, Roxana said nothing. She looked irritated all the time thereafter. Ava, her mother, and sisters were filled with apprehension. None of them had the nerve to tell Shahryar about the insult he had carelessly inflicted.

This ceremony was followed by an exchange of gifts between the families. The groom had requested that this exchange be minimized to a few traditional silver coins. This was duly undertaken. But Shahryar Irani could not restrain himself and followed it up next day with the delivery of a new Dodge car, numerous gold chains, diamond studded watches, clothes, shoes and so on. Roxana returned her gifts the day after. This was the first message delivered directly to Shahryar Irani and the backdrop to what followed.

Ava was married a month later. Soroush Irani arrived at their door in a jama-pichhoir and Ava's mother planted a fresh red kunkun on his forehead. The wedding proceeded with two priests and two witnesses in attendance. After the rice throwing, coconut smashing in front of fire and candles midst chanting of Yatha Ahu Vairya prayer their right hands were joined tightly. Through this simple event Roxana was polite but she kept herself aloof. It was obvious that Soroush was torn, enchanted by the pretty bride looking radiant in white on the one hand and sensible of his sister's disapproval. He was a simple, humble, good-hearted man incapable of giving offence to anyone.

Where would the married couple live! The groom had no house of his own. He lived with his older brother as a bachelor. On that question there was much confusion. That he may live in his father-in-law's house was ruled out first by Roxana and then hastily by Soroush himself. So, they went to the Major General's home in the cantonment where the extended family lived and where the Dodge car was parked till a solution could be found. Following Roxana's example none in the household showed any interest in Ava's parents or their wealth.

That Ava's life changed drastically thereafter can hardly be considered surprising, that it changed for the worse so quickly was quite extraordinary. The house in the cantonment was not large enough for another couple, the children vacated a room for them with the promise that they would recover it soon. They had examinations to study for. Ava had no room, no household duties, no role whatsoever. Roxana had no time for her. She was a busy woman. Ava sensed soon enough that Roxana despised her. The Major General's wife was a fashionable lady with a westernised lifestyle along with western mannerisms but little education. Her husband was too eminent, too busy a man to notice anyone else except his own wife. The wife quickly assessed the new arrival, found Ava rather dull, simple minded, and biddable. She soon became a retiring sort of lady with frequent migraines, who did not stir from her chambers unless to go out, requiring Ava to take over cooking and supervision of the kitchen. She only rose from her torpor when the table was set for dinner, the cutlery misplaced, the meat not well spiced or the dessert not well done.

Ava said nothing, no complaint issued from her lips least of all to her husband. Nor did she say anything to her own family who she visited but infrequently in Bombay. She was brought up to be gentle and timid, and above all follow the path of Asha and that she continued to do. Humata, Huxta, Huvarshta; being good for the sake of goodness without any hope of reward. She repeated these notions to herself every morning in Pune, facing the sun as a readily available source of light. A year passed in which Soroush tried his hand at various trades. Without much success. Ava felt her husband's mounting panic. She recognised their condition as dependents even though they did not speak of it. He was a quiet man, always gentle and kind, increasingly so with her. They vacated the children's bedroom, slept in the living room with no privacy worth the name.

She decided to discuss the situation with her older sister. When Dina heard what Ava's life had become, she was aghast and told her mother. The mother told the father. This circuit of information took many months. By this time Ava delivered a baby boy. Her family celebrated, this time soberly, more cautiously. Shahryar Irani very timidly mentioned to his son-in-law that he was willing to buy a bigger house for the family where they could all live together since that is how they had lived all their lives. The Major General was about to retire, and the army house would have to be vacated gradually. Both families realised that it was a sensible suggestion. Shahryar Irani's family did not have the resources to buy such a large house in a suitable area in or close to the cantonment, but the Major General was firm about putting down half the money.

So, a new house and an improved status was attained for Ava after two long years. It was an improvement over the previous arrangement, but it was by no means comfortable for so many residents. The new house had only one rather primitive toilet.

Nobody had the resources to improve the house and Ava dare not speak of the situation to her own father. Further, it is one thing to have a roof over one's head yet another to put food on the table for a large family. Ava gave birth to one more baby, another boy and after many years the last one came, a girl. They named her Ariana Armani Irani. Armani because Ava had longed for a daughter. Soroush Irani was a proud father of two sons and a daughter. Ava had done her duty. The Major General's wife had produced two daughters but no son.

In the time being, Roxana had resolved to not to let Ava's status rise in the household. From Ava she perceived an imminent threat not only to her own status and to her more modern way of living and thinking. A way that she had tried hard to pass on to the next generation of nieces. Ava's constant prayers, various superstitions, submissiveness, gentleness to the point of lack of firmness with even the servants made her an unlikely role model for the next generation. Her lack of education and absence of good English-speaking skills or any desire to improve herself made Ava an emblem of backwardness, more or less to be rejected. Roxana's indifference to her sons pained Ava more than her indifference to herself had but she said nothing.

Soroush was struggling to establish himself in a trade. Matters were so that Ava feared for her first-born Dinyar, now of school going age. She knew he would not be able to go to a good school like the Major General's children. They had no money for the fees. He would be despised like her for deficiency of education. She began to worry night and day for his wellbeing. Eventually she convinced a reluctant, remorseful Soroush about the seriousness of their position. Then Ava secretly requested her mother to keep the child in Bombay and give him a good education. The pretext she invented for a wider audience was that she was too preoccupied with the younger children to take good care of Dinyar. Thus, little Dinyar left home at the age of five never to return and his mother spent many sleepless nights crying.

Roxana had taken an active interest in the development of the two older girls of the household by admitting them into in the school where she herself taught. She trained them in music, drama encouraged them to read widely and speak clearly and logically. Her influence over them was obvious. History, literature, music, books were the hub of conversation among them. They were growing up into smart, modern, young women who were soon seeking admission into universities in England. Whatever her other failings may have been, Roxana was consistent. She began to take some interest in Armani as soon as she grew out of her diapers and further more as she grew up. The main thing that she repeated to Armani as soon as she could was, "God is manmade, for man's consolation and use alone. Remember 'He' is manufactured by men, not by women like you or me. Women have to be rational, thinking creatures. They pay the most terrible price for being otherwise." Armani had no idea what that meant at the age of ten, but she was to recall it many years later. Just as she was to recall other things about the fearful Roxana.

Eventually, as the older girls left home for England, Armani was admitted into St Mary school. Roxana took good care of her. Concentrating all her energy on Armani, she began to tempt her with books, music, and drama. Although Armani had a lovely singing voice and much talent for the piano she was not as pliable as the older girls from the start. Later she even learned a clear, fearless on stage speaking style. Putting her reading and logic to good use Armani was soon winning medals in inter-school debating contests. As a teenager she began to be recognised as a promising student, a debater, singer, and pianist but her capriciousness also grew. She began to relish a little rebellion as well and a little adventure. On such occasions Roxana was stern maybe too stern with both Ava and Armani. Perhaps she was apprehensive that the mothers influence would eventually hinder Armani.

Armani was too young to know that her rebellion was rooted in an almost subconscious grasping of reality. Her mother continued to be meek, submissive, voiceless in a household where she was now performing all the duties of a mother, sister-in-law, and housekeeper. Her father was making money now, he was the main bread winner yet her oldest brother remained in exile. Since he was excelling at school in Bombay it was agreed by her parents that he must not be disturbed. But Armani noted that Daniyar had grown increasingly alienated from his parents and siblings. His polite coolness made her mother cringe. In her maternal grandparent's home Armani noticed considerably more empathy and generosity of spirit than in Roxana who was a champion of modernism and women's rights. On one occasion, her maternal grandmother had told her of an episode that was to haunt Armani. Apparently at some point Ava had started eating less so that the children could have more food. Armani did not know this till her grandmother told her that Ava had in fact fainted from hunger and since the fainting spells continued a doctor was consulted. The doctors had diagnosed her problem as severe malnutrition. While recalling the past her grandmother had sobbed, "My poor daughter has endured too much, I could have called her back to this house but that it would be inconceivable socially. Married girl did not return to her parents' home alive."

Armani began to notice things. She observed that her second brother, Dara was far less obedient had many more freedoms than any of the girls in the family. No one checked him, least of all Roxana. Roxana's coldness to her mother was relentless, it made Armani indignant. She noted that every time a relative said that Armani was a spitting image of her mother Roxana cringed visibly. This had happened on her Navjot ceremony too she recalled but then she was too young then to understand. Besides Roxana stood so aloof from all religious rituals that her conduct did not get noticed. Roxana did not even answer questions in Dari, she used only English and so Ava was excluded instantly. Roxana did not want to be called Foy only Aunty. Because of her inflexibility the household spoke only in English to each other. All except Ava and her husband. Armani found that the duties of managing the household gave her mother no time for rest and recreation. Armani began, unknowingly, to hope for some sign of rebellion from her mother. But none came. She chatted with her mother on the rare occasions that they were alone or out of the house. At such times they spoke in Dari, Armani complained about Roxana, at other times mentioned the lack of participation in household responsibilities by her aunts, sometimes she talked about the house helps who were torn between different power centers in the household. But her mother seemed to bear no grudge, harboured no despair, no envy, not even a trace of resentment. She had no concept of rights. As though the French Revolution has never occurred and if it had, it left Ava untouched. Ava would instead urge Armani to pray sincerely, speak well of everyone, gently scolding her for having so many bad thoughts about elders. “It is my duty to do the right deeds, to serve,” Ava would say softly and steer the subject to the plight of poor overworked servants at home or poor people on the streets. As though she found some comfort in those more oppressed that herself. And Armani would fall silent because the motto of her school scrolled in bold letters over the threshold, also read, “I serve”. She looked at it everyday.The school was run by British nuns who took the motto rather seriously. Pandita Ramabai and Dr Ida Scudder where role models held up by the school. But all this devotion to endless service without any rationale, this personal, idiosyncratic charity, without addressing issue of equality and fairness to all, left Armani vaguely disappointed. Had you asked her at sixteen what dissatisfied her she would have great difficulty in expressing it comprehensively, yet discontented she was.

Sensing some disgruntlement, Roxana’s vigilance escalated. Her fear increased to the extent that she lost some civility. She started describing Armani’s misdeeds, academic improvements, or lack of them to the family at large. Every so often this would occur over dinner. Only her mother did not participate in such family conversations. The eyes of four adults seemed perpetually fixed on her. Roxana eyes seemed most acute, hurtful, and tyrannical. Armani began to withdraw into herself, stopped eating well, grew pale and thin. At night she often dreamt of a tall, gaunt lady with thick black eyebrows and a cloud of long, thick, black, wavy hair chasing her all over Main Street, East Street, around Empress Garden, through the lanes of the cantonment even as she ran frantically to hide. She would wake up with her heart pounding and in a cold sweat. The dreams recurred. The lady in her dream looked remarkably like Roxana.

Nevertheless, Armani would say many years after she had left the comfort of her Pune home, that it was a relatively happy childhood as childhoods go. As the youngest child of the household she got more attention than anyone else. The older children had gone to study abroad. Her father was at last making some money in spice trade. He indulged her wished. They had always lived in the posh side of town, they owned a big car which her father finally drove because he could afford the fuel, she wore western clothes in the contemporary fashion. She was much envied by her school friends. She had only longed for less supervision, less berating, she had wished her mother would stand up against the haranguing, that her father stood up for his wife. She had wished for more fairness within and outside her home. She had wished for people in her life who had more empathy, people who added happiness to the lives of others. She had felt deeply lonely.

Roxana's coaching in rational thought was so overpowering that romance, boys, fashion, entertainment, marriage did not interest Armani as much as it fascinated her classmates. There were no boyfriends, nothing to take away her loneliness. She was seized with a restlessness that was settling deep into her soul. Armani did not know that she was turning into a rebel. It began as a metaphysical rebellion not just against her condition but against the whole of creation and God who said all were made equal but did nothing to make them equal. God was supervising her but not the tyrants. She felt that the conditions of her existence were intolerable, that she was justified in wishing she had more rights, wishing that her mother had more rights. She wanted to say NO! out loud. No! to Roxana particularly. Roxana who did not introspect, did not assess her own motives in dealing harshly with other women. Roxana who had lost empathy and joy. With all her modern education and rationality she had acquired a dried-up soul. She wanted to stand up to Roxana. But Armani could not find the courage in Pune.

When she finished high school, Armani told her parents that she wanted to go to a college in Bombay. Her brother Daniyar had been sent away, but Armani chose to go, she wanted to go, she begged to go. Daniyar had done brilliantly well. He had gone off to America on a scholarship for higher studies. Her grandparents were growing old, they welcomed her arrival into their empty nest. All the maternal uncles and aunts had moved out and led independent lives. Nobody objected to her arrival. Her parents could find no reason to refuse.

That is how Armani escaped and arrived as a student in Elphinstone college. In the 1970s it was the most sought-after college in Bombay for the study of Humanities and English literature, with a luminous faculty and vibrant student life. In Bombay, she found herself generally in the care of her grand-parents but at great liberty. They were far too old to supervise. In Bombay, she found herself drawn like a horseshoe magnet to Left student politics. There she met the love of her life, found the mission of her life, experienced heart break and met all the people who became fellow travelers. Here her life turned inside out and upside down.

The first time she heard a Left student leader's campus talk she stood still in astonishment. A tall, thin, swarthy, bright-eyed boy was speaking on a makeshift podium. He talked of oppression, inequality, injustice. He seemed to make a few points, then he linked the points and the ideas that emerged seemed to touch a hidden cord in her. She had done enough public speaking as a schoolgirl to realise it was not the style in which it was being said for that was clearly unpolished nor the choice of phrases but what was being said that elevated her. That was a spell binding moment, she could bring it to mind till the day she died.

One of the leaders, Shridhar was particularly bright and persuasive. She tried to read all the books he talked about but there were too many. She read the leaflets he circulated on the issues of the day. Fell utterly in love with him and though how very unlike a dream boy he was. None of her school friends would find him attractive. Others in his circle like Avinash, Travis, Jennifer, Sebastian, Geeta, Abdul were also fine speakers. They formed a band of well informed, well read, supportive, coherent members of the Left student's union. It was intoxicating to be among them. There was a passion, a momentum and it radiated outwards. In the tumultuous times that the 1970s were there was much happening in the country and outside to be debated. Many protests and marches against Vietnam, against inflation, cost of food, hostel fees to mention only a few followed and expanded her consciousness endlessly till it encompassed all of oppressed humanity. Armani was drawn to the warmth that emanated from the energy, it seemed as though she was facing the sun at last. In that collective energy she experienced the end of loneliness for the first time in her young life.

Her education had prepared her for this day perhaps. Swiftly it became apparent to Armani where the roots of injustice lay. It seemed as if she had been staring at it for years but had not seen that injustice was rooted in the unequal access to wealth and resources, in the laws made by the wealthy and powerful who used them to enhance their wealth and oppress the dispossessed. She realised that her mother's obsessive religiosity was simply the sigh of the oppressed. God was the soul in a soulless word! She realised that women without any property to their name, were at the bottom of the pecking order. The wife of the poorest man was poorer than him, she had lesser rights and freedoms than he had. She did not have to look far. Her parent's life was testimony to that. She noticed that low self-esteem was ground into the poor, meek but most of all into women of all social classes. It took years to extract them from that timidness. All of the socio-religious conventions seemed to be constructed to remind them to be fearful, docile, to make oppressive social relations tolerable. Fair relations of exchange needed no complex laws of coercion, but unfair ones did. She understood that no rights could be secured, nothing common to the benefit of many could be achieved alone. Personal charity was necessary, but it was far from enough. Without a collective of many who shared a programme one might as well accept the world and its power structures as they were. Might as well stay meek, rooted in superstitions then become a rebel without a cause, to be eternally bewildered, to be crushed and whipped out. A large and ever enlarging collective that used facts, reason for developing generally, shared values of how society should be was necessary without doubt. It needed a core group that used theory and evidence repeatedly, insistently. The core group needed to grow itself, agitate, educate, and move forward relentlessly for a common goal. All this was imperative.

Her isolation vanished as she became a part of a collective and her comrades became the family she chose. As she grew up in the movement, she found that all families have their woes. At twenty-five Armani realised that the breakaway from the old family had been a lot easier than making of a new family committed to ideals of equality and fairness.

She would say to those of her comrades who despaired, "We are making the new out of the old. Even the new families we choose to become part of. After all the new family is made out of elements of the old families, it is made by others like me trying to escape tyranny. To reimagine everything is an arduous task for the human mind. We are all creatures of mental habits." When she was thirty Armani began to understand why Roxana was trying so hard to control. How can one make something completely new from old material without force and coercion? Yet one must try earnestly, carefully, to make the coercion tolerable for one had to make the new and keep in mind that the alternative is miserable!

At thirty-five, Armani could not explain what was drawing her into the tidal waves that came at her, one after another. Why she was unable to run away from a task that nothing had prepared her for. Instead, she kept leaping right into every tumult. As though compelled by a force beyond her to keep grasping, contending with the complexity of the undertaking she had chosen and not to give up. Going to places where her work took her. She traveled into regions where few Indians had ever been, deep inside rural areas unconnected by roads, through forests, where no buses went, she traveled on donkeys, slept on haystacks, and lived on dry meals. Fell ill in areas where no hospitals existed, no doctor was available. Recovered from repeated bouts of malaria with some difficulty. Struggling again thorough swamps, in intense heat and humidity she would sometimes think of her forefathers who arrived on foot from Iran with only the shirt on his back. Once her grandfather had told her the story. On other occasions she thought of Siddhartha who left this palace and dwelled on the nature and roots of human suffering. But most of the time she would tell her friends and audience, that she thought about and found a validation of Marxist theory she had taken time studied in college.

She watched the sinister nature of capitalism. She saw up close the compounding of human suffering at an inconceivable, unsustainable rate. Dispossession of tens of thousands of tribals, farmers and peasants, land grabbing, mining and dam building, hopelessness, destitution, and arrival into cities, the creation of a planet of slums. She saw the sprawling slums within the metropolis they spread as far as the eye could see. All this happened before her very eyes. Oh! the hollowness of democracy in the midst of raging capitalism. Even the Buddha would have had to reconsider his route, she said. Everywhere she went with her comrades Armani's mission was to inform, educate, embolden, and organise collectives of the marginalised to protect rights that the democratic constitution had granted them. On many such occasions she found herself using drama, song and thinking of Roxana again. Roxana had taught her the art.

At sixty she returned to the old family but only to nurse her aging father, and grievously ill mother. When Armani had refused to go to England to study law Ava had lived calmly through the brickbats that descended on her from everyone in the family but most particularly from Roxana. Armani had continued to live and work in Bombay with the political Left, detached from the old family and unfazed by their disapproval. She had not married, neither had she gone on to a successful career. She studied law in Bombay and taught it off and on. Family, relatives, and friends in Pune thought Armani had gone wildly astray. They whispered that she went about with strange, unkempt people to strange places. They had no hesitation in declaring that Armani had wasted her life. She had been the topic of every Irani community discussion for years! That she who had been the most promising of all the children in the household should waste her life so was attributed to mild manners of the mother and unchecked freedoms in Bombay. Ava did not react to any censure, as was her way. But she never stopped doting on Armani, never accused her of squandering away her life in a futile struggle. Following his wife's example her father accepted Armani's choice with grace. Extending his hospitality to all her comrades, he offered them the best scotch whiskey and food whenever they came calling. Soroush Irani spent his last days in the room he had constructed in the memory of Daniyar, his first born who never returned. He passed away before his frail wife.

Entirely bed ridden in her old age, with her daughter by her side, Ava began to show a keen interest in Armani's work. She wanted to know more about the political groups she worked with. She wanted to know about the education programme among the poor and marginalised. Was often startled and silent for hours after Armani explained matters to some considerable degree. Armani hoped that her mother would come to **understand** her work not just tolerate it. Then one day holding her hand, Ava murmured, "You served too, you severed more and beyond narrow family or community. Give away all the family wealth after I die in a manner you think fit."

Armani nursed her parents devotedly. Balancing the two worlds she had come to know ardently, she served. There was no one else left to do what needed to be done. All the elders were dead, all the siblings, who had received the best education that the country could offer, had flown away abroad and away to greener pastures.